MASQUERADE

MASQUERADE

by Mikhail Lermontov

Translated from the Russian
by Valentina Hine and Robert Leach

First published in Russian as Маскарад in 1873

Proofreading by Richard Coombes

English translation © Valentina Hine and Robert Leach 2025

Cover image: Joseph-Désiré Court, 'Au bal masque
(Vénitienne au bal masqué)' (1837)

www.glagoslav.com

ISBN: 978-1-80484-243-0
ISBN: 978-1-80484-244-7

Published in English by Glagoslav Publications in September 2025

A catalogue record for this book is available from the British Library.

Mikhail Lermontov

MASQUERADE

Translated from the Russian
by Valentina Hine and Robert Leach

GLAGOSLAV PUBLICATIONS

MIKHAIL LERMONTOV

(1814-1841)

Contents

Introduction

'If one were to seek the [Russian] author who best fits the stereotype of "the romantic poet," Mikhail Lermontov would win without question.' So wrote John Mersereau Jr in *The Cambridge History of Russian Literature*, and it is a judgment with which it is hard to disagree, and one which has been shared by most readers and critics since Lermontov's death.

Mikhail Yuryevich Lermontov was born in Moscow in 1814. His mother came from a wealthy family, while his father was in the military. But their marriage seems to have been an unhappy one, and in any case his mother died in 1817. He was raised by his maternal grandmother, but she and Lermontov's father constantly disagreed about his upbringing. His youth was therefore turbulent and difficult, and in his teens his troubles were multiplied by his poor health. He was lonely, melancholy, haughty and even unapproachable. But he did not lack charisma.

He began to write poems, and by the age of fourteen he had already displayed a remarkable precocious talent. For the rest of his short life, he was prolific, creating not only poems, but also plays and novels. In 1830 he enrolled at Moscow University; two years later he joined the Life Guard Hussars; but at all times he continued energetically with his writing. Like so many of the Romantic writers throughout Europe, Lermontov came to admire especially Lord Byron, and in 1840 his novel, *A Hero of our Time*, gave perhaps the most telling expression of any to the Byronic figure. However, it should also be noted that Arbenin, the hero of the play,

Masquerade, was a significant earlier portrayal of that same Romantic Byronic hero.

But Lermontov's was a tangled and ill-fated life. He fought more than one duel, and in July 1841 in Pyatigorsk, he was shot in a duel, and died 48 hours later. He was just twenty-six years old.

He never saw his play, *Masquerade*, performed – the first performance did not take place until the 1860s. It was rejected by the censor on account of the sharpness of its satire, which culminates in the final act when the Lady remarks bluntly that the cause of her cousin's death was 'the stupidity of our society.' Moreover, much of the action of the play takes place in a very real setting – the house of Engelhardt, well-known in the early 1830s for hosting balls and masquerades attended by the upper echelons of society, even including members of the family of the tsar himself. Lermontov certainly attended a few such events there in 1834 and 1835.

The play tells of a gambler and rake, Arbenin, who has been reformed by the love of his innocent young wife, Nina. He thinks that he has discovered that she is unfaithful to him with Prince Zvezdich. He decides to kill the Prince, and when this fails, he tries to humiliate him by throwing a pack of cards in his face in a gambling den. In fact, Nina has not been unfaithful to him: she unknowingly dropped a bracelet at a masquerade. This was picked up by Baroness Shtrall, who gave it to an admirer of hers – Prince Zvezdich. But Arbenin refuses to believe in Nina's innocence, especially when he sees her speaking to the Prince at a society ball. He poisons her ice cream there, and when they return home, he tells her what he has done. She dies. But it is then that a stranger remorselessly reveals the truth to him, thereby driving him to insanity. It is a deliberately *Othello*-like story of unfounded jealousy, with the bracelet taking the place of Othello's handkerchief, though the characters are romantic, not Shakespearean.

It may also be noticed that gambling, such as that shown in *Masquerade*, was a perennially fascinating subject for the Russian intelligentsia of the time. Other treatments of it may be found in Alexander Pushkin's 1835 play, *The Queen of Spades*, which Tchaikovsky later made into the well-known opera; *The Gamblers*, Nikolay Gogol's play of 1840; and *The Gambler* (1866) by Fyodor Dostoyevsky, written very rapidly with the aim, ironically enough, of making enough money to pay off his gambling debts.

The present translation of Lermontov's drama is entitled *Masquerade*, not *The Masquerade*, which is a possible alternative. The reason for this is because the action is not so much realistic as performative. To include 'the' in the title limits the subject; without 'the', the idea of masquerading becomes central. The masquerade is a place where participants are required to perform: the mask removes their usual quotidian person, and compels them to playact. Near the end of the play, Kazarin says to Arbenin, 'Enough of this, brother – take off the mask,' and admits, 'we're both actors.' If, therefore, a masquerade is inherently performative, the actors of Kazarin, Arbenin and the rest must decide how this performativity can be accessed. It asks questions, for example, of how the many 'asides' which the characters speak may be presented. The lack of the article in the title also focuses the question of Arbenin's behaviour – is it the result of demonic possession, as nineteenth century interpreters tended to suggest, or social pressure, as was often adduced in the twentieth century? And who then is the Stranger? The embodiment of some unseen force, or a hired assassin (as the great theatre director, Vsevolod Meyerhold, opined)?

Indeed it was Meyerhold's production in 1917 in St Petersburg which demonstrated this play's extraordinary dramatic power. At least five years in the making, and probably the most expensive production ever mounted in a theatre at that time, the production lasted in the repertoire of the Alexandrinsky Theatre till the 1940s, by which time the director himself had been done to death in one of Stalin's prisons. It was rehearsed and first presented, however, as the revolution was gathering pace, so that even reaching the theatre for the early audiences was extremely hazardous. The leading actor was turned away by soldiers at one early performance, though an officer who had seen him act managed to intervene, and thus enabled him to get through; Meyerhold himself and his designer, Alexander Golovin, had to run through flying bullets on one occasion; and on another, an audience member was actually shot dead at the entrance to the theatre.

But the production survived, and it was able to demonstrate the power of Lermontov's quintessential Romanticism.

Robert Leach

MASQUERADE

Characters

Yevgeny Alexandrovich Arbenin
Nastasya Pavlovna, 'Nina', his wife
Prince Zvezdich
Baroness Shtrall
Afanasy Pavlovich Kazarin
Adam Petrovich Shprikh
The Stranger
Host at the gambling house
A clerk
Sasha, Nina's maid
The Aunt
The Niece
Doctor
Old Man
Gamblers
Servants
Maskers
Guests

The action takes place in St Petersburg in 1835.

ACT ONE

Scene One

A gambling house. Card players: Zvezdich, Kazarin, Shprikh and others at the table, playing; more men standing around.

1 GAMBLER : Ivan Ilich, allow me, please.
BANKER : You're welcome.
1 GAMBLER : One hundred roubles.
BANKER : Certainly.
2 GAMBLER : Very well, begin, please.
3 GAMBLER : The luck's got to change – it's these cards, they're bewitched.
4 GAMBLER : I shall have to double the stakes.
3 GAMBLER : Play.
2 GAMBLER : On that? … No, I'll get burned.
4 GAMBLER : My dear sir, you know that nowadays, unless you are extremely cunning, you can achieve nothing.
3 GAMBLER (*whispering to 1 Gambler*) : Be careful. Keep your eyes on him.
PRINCE : I'm going for broke!
2 GAMBLER : My dear Prince, emotions only poison the blood. Be so good as to remain calm while playing.
PRINCE : Be so good as to keep your advice to yourself.
    (*They play.*)
BANKER : The card is dead.
PRINCE : Hell!
BANKER : Pass all the stakes, please.

2 GAMBLER (*mockingly*) : I see that in the heat of the moment you're ready to lose everything. What price your epaulettes?

PRINCE : Honour was the price – a currency you couldn't pay in.

2 GAMBLER : If I were you, I'd be less chicken-bold – considering your age and your lack of luck!

(*Prince, having drunk a glass of lemonade, sits at the side and falls into contemplation.*)

SHPRIKH (*approaches him sympathetically*) : Is it cash you need, Prince? I would be honoured to help you – my interest is low, and my patience inexhaustible.

(*Prince nods coldly to him and turns away. Shprikh retreats, looking displeased. Arbenin enters, bows to everybody, comes to the table. He signals to Kazarin, and steps aside with him.*)

ARBENIN : Why are you not taking part? Well, Kazarin?

KAZARIN : I'm merely observing. And yes, my dear sir, you are married now, rich – you have become a sybarite, you have even forgotten your friends.

ARBENIN : Well – I haven't been here with you for some time.

KAZARIN : Are you busy?

ARBENIN : Busy making love, not money.

KAZARIN : Escorting your wife to all the balls?

ARBENIN : No.

KAZARIN : Do you still play cards?

ARBENIN : No, that's finished for me. But there are new faces here. Who is that … (*ironically*) … fashion plate?

KAZARIN : Shprikh! Adam Petrovich! I can easily acquaint you with him. (*Shprikh approaches them, and greets them with a bow.*) This is my friend. Let me introduce you. Arbenin.

SHPRIKH : I know you –

ARBENIN : I do not remember our having met –

SHPRIKH : By reputation. Yes, I've heard such a great deal about you that for a long time I've wished to make your acquaintance.

ARBENIN : Unfortunately I never heard anything about you. But I'm sure you yourself will let me hear plenty. (*They bow to each other. Shprikh, making a sour face, retreats.*) I don't like him. I've seen all sorts of faces, but it would take a considerable effort to invent one like that. Look at his smile. He has a vicious smile. Eyes as if they were made of glass. When you look at him, you can't tell whether he's a human being or a devil.

KAZARIN : Well, my dear friend, a person's appearance is not important. Even if he were the devil incarnate, we'd still need him. If one needs money, he instantly obliges. I really have no idea what his nationality is – he speaks all languages. He's probably a Yid. He knows everybody, he's involved in everybody's business. He remembers everything, he knows everything, he's always up to something. He's been thrashed more than once. If he meets an atheist, he behaves like an atheist; if he associates with a saint, he is a Jesuit; when he's with us, he's a gambler; and when he mixes with honest people, he is the most honest person in the world. In other words – I'm sure you'll like him.

ARBENIN : The portrait may be impressive, but the original is odious! Well, what about that tall gentleman with the moustaches and the make-up? A haunter of fashionable shops, certainly, and a retired womanizer? He's blatantly westernized – I'm sure he's a hero of trivialities, yes? He can hit any target of no significance.

KAZARIN : It's almost like that. He was expelled from his first regiment for fighting a duel – or rather, for not fighting it. He was afraid to kill – his mama told him not to. Then, after a few years, he was challenged to another duel, and this time he did fight.

ARBENIN : What about the scruffy little man there, the one with the broad grin and the cross and the little snuff box?

KAZARIN : Trushov. He is a man not fully appreciated: he served in Georgia for seven years, or was despatched there with some general. There he killed somebody – but slyly, not in a duel. He spent five years with this general, and got the cross round his neck as a reward.

ARBENIN : You're obviously very fussy when choosing your friends.

GAMBLERS : Kazarin! Afanasy Pavlovich, come over here!

KAZARIN : I'm coming. (*With affected attention and interest*) What an extraordinary example of treachery. Ha ha ha ha!

1 GAMBLER : Hurry up!

KAZARIN : What happened?

(*The players talk animatedly, then calm down. Arbenin notices Prince Zvezdich and approaches him.*)

ARBENIN : Prince, what are you doing here? Perhaps it isn't your first visit?

PRINCE (*moodily*) : I could ask the same of you.

ARBENIN : I can forestall your question. Many of the people here have been my acquaintance for a long time. I often used to come here and watched anxiously how the wheel of fortune spun. I saw how it uplifted one person to the heights, and dashed another into an abyss. I never envied them, but neither did I feel any sympathy. I just watched them – young people, full of hope and ardour, others happy in their ignorance of life … passionate souls whose lives had been devoted to love – they soon shrivelled here in front of my eyes. Today destiny drew me back to see this again.

PRINCE (*taking him by the arm, emotionally*) : I have lost –

ARBENIN : I know. So what now? Are you going to drown yourself?

PRINCE : Oh, I'm in desperate straits.

ARBENIN : There are only two remedies for that. Either you have to take your oath that you will never gamble again. Or you can go straight back to the table. But to be successful, you'll have to abandon everybody and everything: your relatives, your friends, your honour. You'll have to test your soul as well as your skill. You'll have to become an expert judge of character, to be able to read people's intentions and their thoughts in their faces. You'll have to train your hands for years, and despise everything and everybody, the rules of society, even the laws of nature. You'll have to think the whole day, then play the whole night. You'll never be free from anxiety, but you'll have to make sure that nobody even suspects you of it. You mustn't tremble when a piece of good fortune lands in your lap, and you mustn't blush when people tell you you're a scoundrel.

(*Silence. The Prince, deep in thought, has hardly listened to Arbenin.*)

PRINCE : I don't know what to do now –

ARBENIN : Whatever you please.

PRINCE : Perhaps luck –

ARBENIN : Ah! This is not the place for that.

PRINCE : I have lost everything ... Oh, advise me what to do.

ARBENIN : I can't.

PRINCE : Well ... I will sit.

ARBENIN (*takes him by the arm*) : Wait. I'll sit instead of you. You are young – long ago I was young and inexperienced, impatient like you, and full of pride and thoughtlessness. If only ... if only someone had stopped me at the right moment ... then ... (*He looks at the Prince very attentively, changes his tone.*) Don't hesitate, give me your hand. Rely on me. (*He comes to the table and is given a seat.*) I hope you won't refuse to play with an old hand? I want to see how Fate treats me now – whether she will cast off her former favourite.

KAZARIN : Look, he couldn't resist … he's agitated. (*Quietly*) Don't make a fool of yourself, and expose our generation to them.

GAMBLERS : You're welcome. Your fate is in your own hands. You are the master, we are mere apprentices.

1 GAMBLER (*whispering in the ear of 2 Gambler*) : Be careful. Keep your eyes skinned. I don't like the look of him – there's something dangerous about him. Even my ace could lose to this robber.

(*The game starts. Everyone gathers round the table, there are various exclamations, one or two players leave the table gloomily. Shprikh takes Kazarin on one side.*)

SHPRIKH (*mischievously*) : Look, they're gathered like a storm cloud. Now wait for the thunder.

KAZARIN : He'll frighten them away for a month.

SHPRIKH : Yes, he obviously knows what he's doing.

KAZARIN : He used to.

SHPRIKH : Used to? But now?

KAZARIN : Now? Now he's married, rich … he's become respectable. He looks as gentle as a lamb, but underneath he's still a beast. Anyone who tells me a man can forget his old habits, or conquer his own nature, is a fool. He may pretend he's an angel, but the devil is still there, deep in his soul. And you, my friend (*patting him on the shoulder*) even though you are a child in comparison with him, in you there's a little devil lurking.

(*Two gamblers, talking animatedly, approach them.*)

1 GAMBLER : Well, I told you –

2 GAMBLER : What could I do? Obviously it was a difficult situation. I tried to – you know what. But no luck – all the cards seemed to be preordained. I was humiliated.

KAZARIN (*approaches*) : Well, gentlemen, obviously you hadn't skill enough to survive in that game.

1 GAMBLER : Arbenin is extremely clever.

KAZARIN : Take heart, my friends –

(*General excitement at the table among the players.*)

3 GAMBLER : If this continues, he'll win a hundred thousand
before we know where we are.

4 GAMBLER (*aside*) : Somewhere he'll fail.

5 GAMBLER : We shall see.

ARBENIN (*gets up*) : That's enough.

(*He picks up a pile of gold coins and comes away from the
table. The rest stay there. Kazarin and Shprikh are at the table
as well. Arbenin takes the Prince by the arm without saying
anything and gives him the money. Arbenin is pale.*)

PRINCE : I won't forget that. You've saved my life.

ARBENIN : And I've saved your money as well. (*Bitterly*)
Sometimes it's difficult to tell which is more precious,
life or money.

PRINCE : But you actually sacrificed yourself for me.

ARBENIN : On the contrary, I was glad of an excuse to make
the blood course through my veins again, to feel my whole
being tingle with excitement. I went to that table as easily
as you would go into battle.

PRINCE : You could have lost.

ARBENIN : Me? Never! Those prodigal days are past. I know
everything – all their devices and subtleties – that's why I
don't play any more.

PRINCE : You are just trying to avoid my gratitude to you.

ARBENIN : To be honest, I can't stand it. Never in my life
have I been obliged to anybody, and even if I did someone
a good turn, I didn't do it because I felt attached to them,
or sympathetic, I did it because it was useful to me.

PRINCE : I can't believe that.

ARBENIN : Nobody's making you believe it. I'm used to people's disbelief from the old days. If I wasn't so lazy, I could
grow into a hypocrite. But enough of that. (*After a pause.*)
You need entertainment. Well, this is a festive season – I
believe there is a masked ball at Engelhardt's.

PRINCE : Yes.

ARBENIN : Shall we go?

PRINCE : With pleasure.

ARBENIN (*aside*) : In the crowds of people I can rest from my thoughts.

PRINCE : There will be women there … beautiful women … and they say there are even –

ARBENIN : Well, let them say so. What then? Under a mask, all ranks are equal. A mask has no soul, it has no rank, it's merely a presence. And putting a mask over your face means you can take it off your feelings.

(*They go.*)

1 GAMBLER : He gave up precisely when it suited him … what an awkward swine!

2 GAMBLER : He didn't even give us time to get our breath.

SERVANT (*appears*) : Supper is served.

HOST : Gentlemen, you are welcome to the table, and I hope the champagne will soften the blows of fate.

(*They all go out.*)

SHPRIKH (*alone*) : I'd like to get closer to Arbenin … and I'd like a free meal tonight as well. (*Putting his finger to his forehead*) Well, I'll have supper here – I'll probably discover something – and follow them to the masquerade afterwards.

(*He goes out, talking to himself.*)

Scene Two

The masquerade. People in masks promenade about the stage. Arbenin stands at one side.

ARBENIN : In vain do I seek entertainment. The multi-coloured crowd passes before my eyes, but my heart remains cold and my imagination is fast asleep. They are all strange to me, and I am strange to them. (*The Prince approaches him, yawning.*) This is the present generation. When I was his age, did I look like that? (*To the Prince*) Well, Prince? Have you found any adventures yet?

PRINCE : No, and I've been here a whole hour!

ARBENIN : Well, you want happiness to catch you. It's certainly a novel idea. Perhaps it could be disseminated through society.

PRINCE : All these masks are so stupid.

ARBENIN : Quite the contrary. A mask is not stupid. First, it's silent, mysterious … when it speaks, it's enticing. Your imagination can add to the words a smile, a glance, whatever you want. For example, look there. How intriguing that tall woman in the Turkish dress looks … how full-bodied she is. Look how her breast throbs passionately – freely. *And do you know who she is?* Perhaps out of her mask she is a princess or a countess, haughty, cold. She is a Diana in society, but Venus at the masquerade. And so perhaps this evening this beauty can be yours for half an hour. And whatever happens – well, you won't greatly suffer!

(*Arbenin walks away. The Prince stands, looks thoughtful.*)

PRINCE : That's true. It sounds wonderful when one talks about it … But I'm still yawning … Oh – here comes one … I wish …

(*A masked lady comes up to him and touches him on the shoulder.*)

MASK : I know … who you are.

PRINCE : Very intimately, obviously.

MASK : And what you're thinking about – I even know that.

PRINCE : In that case, you are happier than I am. (*He tries to unmask her.*) But if I'm not mistaken, there's a pretty mouth –

MASK : If you find me attractive, so much the worse.

PRINCE : For whom?

MASK : For one of us.

PRINCE : I don't see why. You won't frighten me with your predictions of doom. I may not have much experience in such matters, but I will discover who you –

MASK : Then you will probably also discover where this conversation will end.

PRINCE : We shall talk, and we shall part.

MASK : Really?

PRINCE : You will go one way, I another.

MASK : What if I am only here for you, to see you and talk to you? What if I tell you that an hour from now you will swear to me that you will never forget me as long as you live, that you will gladly give up your life for me, just to hear from my lips, at the moment of parting – 'till we meet again'?

PRINCE : You're clever, mask. But your words are wasted. If you know me, then tell me who I am.

MASK : You? Indecisive, immoral, atheistic, conceited, evil but weak. In fact, the mirror of this age, this present age which glistens on the surface but is hollow within. Is that you? Wanting a meaning in your life, but at the same time afraid of passion and feelings. Wanting to have everything, but not knowing how to sacrifice anything. Despising people without pride or without emotions, but at the same time being a toy in their hands. Oh, I know the type ...

PRINCE : Well, I'm very flattered.

MASK : You've done much wrong –

PRINCE : Unintentionally, perhaps –

MASK : Who knows? I only know a woman shouldn't fall in love with you.

PRINCE : I'm not looking for a love affair.

MASK : You don't know how to look for one.

PRINCE : I'm rather tired of looking for it.

MASK : But if she appears before you and tells you – 'You are mine,' will you dare to be indifferent?

PRINCE : And who is she? Of course, Ideal Woman.

MASK : No, just a woman ... does more than that matter?

PRINCE : But show her to me, let her be so bold as to appear.

MASK : You want so much. Think what you have said. (*Pause.*) She doesn't demand sighs, or compliments, no tears, no pleas or emotional speeches ... But one thing you must promise – abandon all efforts to discover who she is ... and be silent about everything.

PRINCE : I swear by the earth and by heaven, and on my honour.

MASK : Very well. Then it may be. But remember, there is to be no trifling between us.
(*They go out, arm-in-arm. Arbenin enters with two male masks. He drags one of them by the arm.*)

ARBENIN : The things you've said, my dear sir, my honour won't allow to let pass. Do you know who I am?

MASK : I know who you used to be.

ARBENIN : Take off your mask – now! You are behaving dishonestly.

MASK : Why? My face is as strange to you as my mask – and I am seeing you for the first time.

ARBENIN : Humbug! You are afraid of me. You're not worth
     my anger. You coward – be off!
MASK : Farewell, then. But beware – unhappiness will befall
     you tonight.
(*He disappears into the crowd.*)
ARBENIN : Stay! He's gone … Who was he? God has played
     a trick on me … It was probably some cowardly enemy.
     There are endless numbers of them. Ha ha ha. Farewell,
     friend, *bon voyage!*
(*Two female masks are sitting on the settle. A man approaches
and makes a pass at one of them, taking her hand. She with-
draws it and departs. A bracelet falls from her wrist onto the
floor.*)
SHPRIKH (*appears*) : Yevgeny Alexandrovich, who was that
     you were dragging along so mercilessly?
ARBENIN : Oh, that was just a joke with a friend.
SHPRIKH : It seems he took your joke pretty seriously. As
     he went, he was cursing you.
ARBENIN : To whom?
SHPRIKH : Another mask.
ARBENIN : I envy your sharpness of hearing.
SHPRIKH : I do hear a lot, but I keep quiet about what I hear.
     I'm not one to poke my nose into other people's affairs.
ARBENIN : That's obvious. So you don't know – what a
     shame – you don't know that –
SHPRIKH : What?
ARBENIN : No, well – it was just a joke …
SHPRIKH : Please tell me –
ARBENIN : They say your wife is a fine relishy dame.
SHPRIKH : Well, what then?
ARBENIN (*changing his tone*) : And that a dark handsome
     man with moustachios frequents your house.
(*Arbenin goes out, whistling a tune.*)
SHPRIKH (*alone*) : May your mouth parch and crack. Very
     well, mock me, but you yourself may yet grow horns.

(*He disappears into the crowd. First Mask enters quickly and excitedly, and falls on a sofa.*)

MASK : Ah! … I can hardly breathe … he was pursuing me all the way. What if he were to remove my mask …? No, he hasn't recognized me. Well, how could he suspect that the woman who is the envy of the *beau monde* could in a moment of passion throw herself on his neck, pleading to him for two sweet moments, not demanding love, merely hoping for pity? Could he suspect who it was who said, 'I am yours'? He will never penetrate this mystery. Let him … I don't want … but he wants something from me, some trinket to remember him by. If … oh, a ring … if I give him a ring … no, I can't … it's too great a risk. (*She looks on the ground and sees the bracelet. She picks it up.*) What a piece of luck. My God! Someone dropped their bracelet. It's enamelled, and gold … I'll give him this. How neat. Let him find me with this.

(*The Prince, with lorgnette, comes hurrying through the crowd.*)

PRINCE : Ah ha … here she is, I could recognize her among thousands. (*He sits beside her and takes her hand.*) You cannot run away now.

MASK : I'm not running away. What do you want?

PRINCE : I want to see you.

MASK : What a comical notion. I'm in front of you.

PRINCE : That is an unkind joke. You obviously want to joke, but I want something else. If you refuse to reveal your divine features this time, I will tear off your treacherous disguise, I will force you …

MASK : How should I understand you? You are dissatisfied … the fact of my love is not enough for you, you want more … you want to desecrate my honour, and then one day, when you meet me at a ball or when I'm taking my promenade, you can snigger with your friends about the little adventure you had with me. And to prove it, you'll say, 'There she is,' and point your finger at me.

PRINCE : I will remember your voice.

MASK : You think so? Hundreds of women have voices like mine. But if you make advances to one of them, you will be mocked at, you will be put to shame, and then you will get your deserts.

PRINCE : But my happiness remains incomplete –

MASK : Does it? Perhaps you should thank your fate that I don't wish to remove my mask. Or perhaps I am old and ugly, and if you saw my face you'd scowl at it.

PRINCE : You want to put me off, but knowing half your charms, I can guess at the rest.

MASK (*making to go*) : Thank you. Farewell.

PRINCE : Oh, stay for a moment! Could you not leave me some token by which I will remember you? Have you no pity for my frenzy?

MASK (*stepping away from him*) : Very well, I will take pity. Here – my bracelet.
(*She throws the bracelet down, and while he is trying to pick it up, she disappears into the crowd.*)

PRINCE (*scanning the crowd vainly for her*) : What a fool I am … This will ravish my reason. (*Seeing Arbenin*) Ah …

ARBENIN (*deep in thought*) : Who was that prophet of doom? … He must know me … I can't think it was a joke.

PRINCE (*coming to him*) : I have taken your advice.

ARBENIN : I'm glad.

PRINCE : But do you know – happiness came by itself –

ARBENIN : Yes, happiness always comes like that.

PRINCE : But the moment I grasped that happiness, and thought I had it in my hand, then – (*He blows on the palm of his hand.*) Now I know that it wasn't a dream, I'm an utter fool.

ARBENIN : I don't know what happened, so I can't disagree with that.

PRINCE : You always make light of things. Shall I give you an inkling? I will, I'll tell you everything. (*He whispers in*

Arbenin's ear.) But it took me by surprise! She ran away from me, and here – (*he shows the bracelet*) this is all that's left. What an anticlimax!

ARBENIN (*smiling*) : And you had begun so successfully. Wait a moment … may I see this bracelet? It's pretty. I've seen it somewhere. Wait … no no … I think I … I can't remember …

PRINCE : Where can I find her?

ARBENIN : You can find another just the same. There are plenty of women like her here, you don't have to search to find them.

PRINCE : But if it's not her? –

ARBENIN : What does that signify? … Just imagine …

PRINCE : No, I will seek her, even at the bottom of the sea. The bracelet will show me the way.

ARBENIN : Very well. Let us each do a tour of the rooms and look for her – but if she is not entirely a fool, she'll be gone by now.

(*They go out.*)

Scene Three

Arbenin's house: the sitting room. Arbenin enters.

ARBENIN : Well, the evening is over. I'm glad. At last I can have a moment's rest. All that motley crowd, all that masquerade, is still running in my mind. The things I've done tonight are laughable. I gave advice to a lover, treated his wildest dreams seriously, searched for the pair to a bracelet! I conjured fantasies as if I were a poet – my God, that role is hardly suitable for someone my age. (*Enter Servant with candle.*) The mistress has returned?

SERVANT : No, sir.

ARBENIN : When is she expected?

SERVANT : She said she would return soon after eleven.

ARBENIN : And it's already half past one. I hope she's not going to stay all night.

SERVANT : I don't know –

ARBENIN : As if you didn't. Very well, go. Leave the candle on the table. I'll call you if I need you. (*Servant goes. Arbenin sits in the armchair.*) God is just! Now I am condemned to distress and desolation for all the sins of my younger days. It used to be other people's wives who waited for me; now it's my turn to wait for my wife. I wasted my youth in the company of sweet, faithless women. I lit fires of love, but never loved myself. No sooner had I started a love affair than I knew how it would finish. I used to repeat the words of love as a nanny repeats fairy tales to her children, till I realized how burdensome it was, how tedious … And then it was suggested to me – get married. Then I could have a holy right not to be involved in love any more. So I found a charming creature. She was beautiful, tender as a lamb, and I led her to the altar. And suddenly inside myself heard a forgotten sound – I searched within my dead soul, and realized I was in love with her. And to my great shame, I was horrified. Again dreams, again love, in my empty soul. I was like an old hulk, back floating on the rough seas again. And where is the harbour now? (*He falls to thinking. Nina enters on tiptoe behind him, and kisses him on the forehead.*) Ah, good evening, Nina … at last. It's high time you were home.

NINA : Is it so late?

ARBENIN : Well, I've been waiting for a whole hour.

NINA : Really? Oh, how sweet of you.

ARBENIN : And you are thinking, The fool, he's sitting waiting, while I –

NINA : Oh, my God! … You are always ill-tempered. You always look discontented, nothing pleases you. When you are away from me, you miss me; when we are together, you are constantly grumbling. Simply say to me – 'Nina, abandon the *beau monde*. I will live with you and for you. You don't need other people, you don't need the empty and superfluous creatures who occupy all your time from morning till night, while I only have the chance to be with you long enough for us to exchange a couple of words.' Say it, and I'll be ready. I am ready now to bury my youth out of town. I won't attend any more balls, I'll give up attempting to follow the dictates of fashion. I'll abandon this boring freedom that I have. Just tell me as if you were telling a friend. … Oh, I've been carried away by my imagination. Very well. Suppose you love me, your love must be small if you are not even jealous of me.

ARBENIN (*smiling*) : Who knows? I used to lead a life of freedom … for me to be jealous – that would be laughable.

NINA : Of course it would.

ARBENIN : And are you angry about that?

NINA : No, I'm grateful.

ARBENIN : You look sad.

NINA : I only tell you that you don't love me.

ARBENIN : Nina.

NINA : Yes?

ARBENIN : Listen. The fetters of fate have bound us together eternally ... Perhaps it was a mistake ... neither you nor I can judge that. (*He takes her to himself and sits her on his lap. He kisses her.*) You are young in your age and in your heart, and as yet you have only read the title page in the Book of Life. The huge sea of happiness and grief is still there before you – you can steer any course. You can still hope, you can still dream your dreams, because the future is full of promise, and your past life is pure. Without knowing your own heart, and without knowing mine, you gave yourself to me and you love me – I believe that. You love me unquestioningly, accepting your feelings like a child. But my love is different. I have seen everything, endured everything, understood and known it all. Often I used to love, more often I used to hate, and most of all I used to suffer. At first I wanted everything, then I despised everything, sometimes I couldn't understand myself, sometimes the world couldn't understand me. My life was cursed, and I withdrew from the feelings and joys of this earth. So many years passed like that. Even now I am quite mortified when I think about the days of my self-indulgent youth. At first I couldn't appreciate you properly – fool – but soon the hard crust on my soul peeled away and an inexpressibly lovely world opened before my eyes. And not in vain, because I was resurrected into life and goodness. And even now my evil angel sometimes carries me away back to the past, rubs from my memory your pure glance and your divine voice. In these moments I am battling with myself. I am afraid to desecrate you with my touch, and I am afraid that you will be frightened if I moan out my anguish. It is then, in these moments, that you tell me I don't love you.

(*She looks at him affectionately, strokes his hair.*)

NINA : You are a strange man. When you talk about your love like that and when I see that you are burning in the flames and I can read your thoughts in your eyes, then I believe everything without any doubts. But very often –

ARBENIN : Often?

NINA : No no, sometimes –

ARBENIN : I'm old in my heart, but you are young. But we could share the same feelings. Remember, when I was your age, I believed everything absolutely.

NINA : Again you are not pleased. Oh my God!

ARBENIN : Oh no … I'm happy, I'm happy … I know I'm cruel, mad, slanderous; but far away, far away from this mob of evil and envious people, I could be happy, I'd be with you. Let's forget about the past … let's send what's past to oblivion … I know that the creator sent you as a reward to me.

(*He kisses her hand, and suddenly notices that there is no bracelet on her wrist. He stops and turns pale.*)

NINA : You've gone pale, you're shivering. Oh God.

ARBENIN : Me? Not at all. Where is your other bracelet?

NINA (*lightly*) : Lost.

ARBENIN : Lost?

NINA : What's the matter? Is it such a great loss? It only cost about twenty-five roubles.

ARBENIN (*to himself*) : Lost … Why am I so anxious about this? My suspicion whispers something very very strange. Was my life with her only a dream? And am I now awakened from its sweetness?

NINA : Truly, I cannot understand you.

ARBENIN (*looking at her piercingly and folding his arms*) : So –
the bracelet is lost?

NINA (*offended*) : No, I'm telling you a lie.

ARBENIN (*to himself*) : Very like, very like.

NINA : I probably dropped it in the carriage. Give order for
the carriage to be searched. Of course, if I'd known it was
going to be like this, I would never have put it on.

ARBENIN (*rings bell; Servant enters*) : Go and search the car-
riage. Search it thoroughly. A bracelet has been lost in it.
And God help you if you come back without it. (*Servant goes.
To Nina*) My honour and my happiness are in the balance.
(*After a pause.*) What if he doesn't find the bracelet there?

NINA : Then it's probably somewhere else.

ARBENIN : Somewhere else? Where? Do you know?

NINA : I've never seen you so mean before, so stern. To put
your mind at rest, I will order a new one exactly like it
tomorrow.

(*Servant enters.*)

ARBENIN : Well? Be quick!

SERVANT : I searched the whole carriage, sir.

ARBENIN : And ... ? You haven't found it?

SERVANT : No ...

ARBENIN : I knew it. Go away. (*He looks at her intensely.*)

SERVANT : Perhaps it was lost at the masquerade –

ARBENIN : Ah! The masquerade! So that was where you
went? (*To the Servant*) Leave me. (*Servant goes. To Nina*)
Why wouldn't you tell me about this before? I'm sure if I'd
known you were going to the masquerade, I would have
claimed the honour of escorting you there, and bringing
you back home. I wouldn't have inconvenienced you by
keeping a strict watch on you while you were there, I
wouldn't have pestered you with my vulgar attentions.
Who were you with?

NINA : You can make enquiries. Anyone will tell you all there
is to tell. They will explain to you in detail who I was with,

who I talked to, who I bestowed my bracelet on as a keep-sake. You can discover everything about the masquerade quite easily, and a hundred times better than if you'd been there yourself. (*She laughs.*) This is a grand joke! My God! How can you make such an unpleasant scene out of nothing? (*She laughs again.*)

ARBENIN : God send that this is not your last laughter.

NINA : Oh, if you carry on like this, it won't be.

ARBENIN : Who knows, perhaps... Listen, Nina, I know I'm laughable, because I adore you profoundly, as only a man can. Do you find that strange? Other people are obsessed with their plans and ambitions: they try to achieve wealth, or are immersed in science, they pursue their careers or medals of office or glory, or else they are caught up in the social whirl, or they travel or gamble. I have travelled, I have gambled, I've been idle and hardworking. I know what friends are worth, and what perfidious love is. I didn't strive for titles and I have not achieved glory, and, rich or poor, I was always bored. Everywhere I saw nothing but evil... but I was too proud to let it affect me. So what is there left in my life? – You. A weak creature, a beautiful angel – Your love, your smile, your look, your breath. I am a human being while I still possess them. But without them, I am deprived of happiness and of my soul, feelings, my existence even. But if I have been deceived... if I have been deceived... if my breast has given warmth to a snake... if I have guessed the truth... if I've been put off my guard by your caresses while another was making a fool of me behind my back... Listen, Nina, I was born with a fiery heart, my feelings are like lava – hard as rock, but when the rock melts, there is no joy in the path of the molten flow. Don't anticipate forgiveness. I won't look to the law to furnish my revenge – I myself without remorse or tears will tear out two lives.

(*He tries to take her by the hand, but she draws back hastily.*)

NINA : Don't come near me … you look horrible!

ARBENIN : Really? Horrible? No, you're joking – I look fool-ish. Yes, laugh, you can laugh … but having done your dirty deed, why bother to look pale and tremble? Come on, where is he, this fervent lover of yours? The glory of the masquerade, let him come here and enjoy his laugh at me. You have given me to taste all the torments of hell, except this one, the last one –

NINA : I see. That's what your suspicion is? And a bracelet is the cause of that? Believe me, your behaviour deserves to be laughed at, not just by me, but by the whole of society.

ARBENIN : Yes, carry on, laugh at me! You fools, light-heart-ed, pitiable husbands, whom in times past I used to de-ceive, you who live as innocent as the saints in paradise … But, oh, you are my paradise, innocent in heaven and on earth … Farewell, I know everything. (*To her*) Away from me, hyena! What a fool I was to think that you would be touched by my misery, would open everything to me, would fall on your knees, filled with remorse at what you had done. I wouldn't be so implacable if I saw just one tear, one … but no, laughter was your answer.

NINA : I don't know who's been slandering me, but I forgive you. I don't feel any guilt. I'm sorry that I can't indulge you, but I won't lie just for your gratification.

ARBENIN : Be silent … that's enough … please.

NINA : But listen – I'm not guilty – I haven't done anything. God can punish me, listen –

ARBENIN : I know in advance what you're going to say.

NINA : These reproaches sting me cruelly. I love you, Yevg-eny.

ARBENIN : Oh, my God! What a moment to declare your love.

NINA : Listen, I beg you. What do you want?

ARBENIN : Revenge.

NINA : Who do you want to revenge?

ARBENIN : Oh, the time will come and you will all be sur-
prised.
NINA : You are going to take your revenge on me? Then
what are you waiting for?
ARBENIN : Playing the heroine doesn't suit you.
NINA (*scornfully*) : Who are you going to wreak your revenge
on then?
ARBENIN : You are afraid for somebody?
NINA : Will I have many moments like this in my life? Please,
stop it. You will kill me with your jealousy. I can't plead
with you, this is impossible ... I can still forgive you.
ARBENIN : Don't trouble yourself.
NINA : But there is a God, He will not forgive.
ARBENIN : I pity you. (*She goes out in tears. Arbenin is left
alone.*) Such is woman! Oh, I know everything, it's all
perfectly familiar to me. I know you all, all your caresses
and reproaches. But how puny that knowledge seems
now – and what a price I'm paying for these lessons. And
indeed – why should she love me? Just because I can put
on this fearsome voice and appearance? (*He goes to her
door and listens.*) What is she doing in there? She's probably laughing. No, she's crying. (*Moving away from the
door.*) What a pity it's too late.
(*He goes out.*)

ACT TWO

Scene One

The Baroness is sitting in her chair, looking tired. She puts her book aside.

BARONESS : I must think. What are we living for? Simply to be able to suit somebody else's taste? Or to be somebody else's slave? George Sand is right. What is a woman nowadays? A creature without will. A toy for the passions or the whims of others. Having a world of judges, but no defenders, she must hide the fire of her passions, or stamp them down. What is a woman? From youth she is decked out to be sold as a sacrificial lamb. Yet she is accused of self-love, and is prohibited from bestowing her favours where she likes. In her breast passions may flame, and if she should one day ignore the rules of society and indulge her feelings, then her well-being and her peace are gone: society pounces on her instantly, unable to acknowledge secret longings. Society judges her honest or vicious according to her demeanour and her dress, and it never forgives her if its notions of propriety have been offended, and it is cruel in its punishment. (*She tries to read.*) No, I can't read ... I am distracted by this one thought. I fear him as if he were my enemy ... when I recall what passed between us, I still can't conquer my surprise. (*Enter Nina.*) Oh!

NINA : *Bonjour.* I've been sledging, and I thought I'd come and call on you, *mon amour.*

BARONESS : *C'est une idée charmante, vous en avez toujours.* (*They sit down together.*) Somehow you look paler than usual, my dear, in spite of the wind and the frost. You've got red eyes – I hope not from tears?

NINA : I slept badly last night, so I'm not well today.

BARONESS : Your doctor mismanages you – you should change him. (*Prince Zvezdich enters.*) Ah, Prince –

PRINCE : Good morning. I called yesterday to tell you that our picnic will not be possible.

BARONESS : Please be seated, Prince –

PRINCE : I wagered before I came in that you would be upset by my news, but you seem quite unmoved.

BARONESS : Well, it is a pity –

PRINCE : I'm very pleased – I'd give twenty picnics for a single masquerade.

NINA : Were you at the masquerade yesterday?

PRINCE : Yes, I was.

BARONESS : Dressed as what?

NINA : There were so many –

PRINCE : Yes, under the masks I recognized some of our ladies. Of course, ladies always enjoy being disguised. (*He laughs.*)

BARONESS (*ardently*) : I can assure you, Prince, that that kind of slander is not at all amusing. How can a scrupulous woman venture to be present at such an event, when all kinds of hoi polloi are there, and any frivolous dunderhead can insult you or laugh at you? And when you run the risk of being unmasked? You should be ashamed of yourself, you should retract what you said.

PRINCE : I can't retract what I said, but I will agree to be ashamed.
(*Clerk enters.*)

BARONESS : Ah! Where have you come from?

CLERK : I just came over from the office to discuss your little business.

BARONESS : Have matters been finally settled?
CLERK : Not completely yet. But perhaps I have come at an
    inopportune moment?
BARONESS : No no.
    (*She walks away with the Clerk towards the window and en-
    gages him in conversation.*)
PRINCE (*aside*) : Now is my chance for an explanation. (*To
    Nina*) I saw you today out shopping.
NINA : Where?
PTINCE : In the English shop.
NINA : When?
PRINCE : Just now.
NINA : I'm surprised that I didn't notice you.
PRINCE : You were engrossed.
NINA (*quickly*) : I was looking for a bracelet. (*She takes one
    from her reticule.*) The pair to this one.
PRINCE : What an attractive bracelet – but where is its fellow?
NINA : Lost.
PRINCE : Really?
NINA : What is surprising about that?
PRINCE : And can you tell me when?
NINA : The other day, yesterday, perhaps last week – why
    do you want to know?
PRINCE : There's some idea in my mind … a strange notion
    perhaps … (*Aside*) Obviously she feels uneasy, and the
    question alerts her. Oh my God – these modest women!
    (*To her*) Perhaps I could volunteer my services to you …
    we could both search for it.
NINA : Thank you … but where?
PRINCE : Where was it lost?
NINA : I can't remember.
PRINCE : Somewhere at the ball?
NINA : Perhaps – it might have been.
PRINCE : It might have been given to somebody as a keep-
    sake?

NINA : What makes you think that? Who could I give it to? My husband?

PRINCE : As if there is only one person in the world – your husband! I have no doubt you have plenty of lady friends. Very well, say it is lost – what about the man who finds it? What will he get as a reward?

NINA (*smiling*) : He will have to wait and see.

PRINCE : But if he loved you – if he found in you his elusive dream – for one smile, one word from you, he would give anything in the world? What if you yourself had dared to give him a hint about future delights, if you yourself, *incognito* behind a mask, had caressed him with sweet words? … Oh, you must understand.

NINA : After what you have just said, I can only understand that you have forgotten yourself. Consequently, I ask you, once and for all, never to speak to me again.

PRINCE : Oh God – I was dreaming … Are you angry? (*To himself*) You've squirmed out of it this time … But wait … the time will come …

(*Nina moves away to the Baroness. Clerk bids farewell and leaves.*)

NINA : *Adieu, ma chère* – until tomorrow.

BARONESS : Wait, *mon ange*, we haven't even exchanged two words.

(*They kiss.*)

NINA (*leaving*) : I will expect you tomorrow.

BARONESS : The day will seem like a week to me.

(*Nina goes.*)

PRINCE (*aside*) : I will have my way. Such modesty! I'm a fool. It may be that she will try to squirm out, but I recognized the bracelet.

BARONESS : You are pensive, Prince?

PRINCE : Yes, there is so much to ponder on.

BARONESS : But your conversation a moment ago was not ponderous – what were you talking about?

PRINCE : I mentioned who I saw at the masquerade.

BARONESS : Who?

PRINCE : Her.

BARONESS : What, Nina?

PRINCE : Yes … I proved it to her.

BARONESS : You have no shame. You are content to repeat slanders to a person's face?

PRINCE : I venture to, sometimes, out of devilment.

BARONESS : Please, have mercy on her, at least in her absence. Besides, you have no proof of it.

PRINCE : No. But yesterday I was given a bracelet, and she has the pair to it.

BARONESS : And you think that is proof? What logic! Every shop has them.

PRINCE : I've just been through them all and discovered that there have only ever been two.

(*Pause.*)

BARONESS : Tomorrow I will give Nina some good advice – not to trust gossips.

PRINCE : And what advice will you give me?

BARONESS : You? To proceed with what you began so successfully. And to cherish more the honour of ladies.

PRINCE : For this double advice – double thanks.

(*He bows, and goes out.*)

BARONESS (*alone*) : How can he tamper with a lady's honour? If I had opened the truth to him, the same would have happened to me. So farewell, Prince. It is not I who will release you from your delusion. Oh no, God forbid. It's strange – how could I find her bracelet? So Nina was there – that's the key to the riddle … I don't know why, but I still love him. Perhaps out of boredom or disappointment, perhaps out of jealousy … I feel restless, dissatisfied with everything. In my imagination, I hear the contemptuous laughter of the shallow world, yet also the whisper of tormenting pity. No, I will save myself, and she can

pay the price. I will save myself from this shame, even if
the consequence is misery. (*She falls to thinking.*) Such an
unaccountable chain of events ...
(*Shprikh enters and bows to her.*)

BARONESS : Oh, Shprikh, as always you arrive at just the
right moment.

SHPRIKH : Thank you. I was always glad to be of service to
you. Your late husband –

BARONESS : You are courtesy personified, as always.

SHPRIKH : ... the Baron, of blessed memory –

BARONESS : About five years ago, I remember.

SHPRIKH : Borrowed a thousand –

BARONESS : I know, and I can pay you the interest on it
immediately.

SHPRIKH : Oh, it's not that I need the money – excuse me – it
just strayed into my mind by chance –

BARONESS : Then tell me what is new in the world.

SHPRIKH : I've just been at the Count's, so I've heard a good
deal. I only left a moment ago. The whole of society is
buzzing with stories.

BARONESS : You've heard all about Prince Zvezdich and
Arbenin, then?

SHPRIKH (*in bewilderment*) : No ... I heard that ... of course ...
no – I think the whole of society was buzzing about that,
but has forgotten about it by now. (*Aside*) I have not the
faintest idea what I'm talking about.

BARONESS : Ah well, if the whole of society has buzzed
about it, there's nothing left for us to say.

SHPRIKH : But I would like to know your opinion, what do
you think about it?

BARONESS : The whole of society has condemned them.
I could give them some advice. To him I would say that
what women appreciate most in a man is persistence:
women like men to surmount a myriad of obstacles to
achieve their target. And to her I would say, be less cen-

sorious, and more modest. Farewell, Monsieur Shprikh. I have an invitation to dine at my sister's, or I would have been delighted to remain longer with you. (*Aside*) Now I am saved – what a lesson I have learned.

(*She goes out.*)

SHPRIKH (*alone*) : Never fret, my lady, I understand your hint. There was no need to tell me twice. How quick-witted and subtle she is. There is intrigue here – I will get myself involved. Then the Prince will be grateful to me. I will put him in my debt … and I can fly here with the latest developments … and perhaps obtain my five years' worth of interest.

(*He goes.*)

Scene Two

Arbenin's study. Arbenin alone.

ARBENIN : Everything is clear to my jealousy – but there
is no proof! I fear a mistake – I can't endure it – should
I allow it to pass as a momentary nightmare … ? Such a
life would be more horrifying than the grave. Bliss in life
belongs to those whose souls have grown chill, who sleep
peacefully through thunderstorms. That is the life I envy.
(*Enter Servant.*)

SERVANT : There is someone below. He's brought a note
from the Princess for the mistress.

ARBENIN : From which Princess?

SERVANT : I couldn't make it out –

ARBENIN : A note? To Nina?
(*He goes out. Servant remains. Enter Kazarin.*)

SERVANT : The master has just this moment walked out.
Will you wait?

KAZARIN : Certainly.

SERVANT : I will inform him you are here. (*He goes out.*)

KAZARIN : I can wait for a year for you any time, Monsieur
Arbenin, and I will wait. I'm in such straits that it is af-
fecting my temper. I need a skilful collaborator. My hopes
of him spring from his habitual magnanimity, and a little
from the fact that he has three thousand serfs as well as the
patronage of the nobility. I need to drag Arbenin back into
gambling, make him resurrect the old days. Then he can
support his old partner – he won't tremble before these

upstart puppies. The youth of this generation cut me like a knife. However you coach them, they will still know nothing. They know neither when to start nor when to stop. They are ignorant of the proper time to be honest, and equally of whom nobly to cheat. Just glance at the older generation: how many of them achieved high rank through gambling? From the dirt they raised themselves to the level of the aristocracy, and how did they do this? By retaining their respectability at all times, by observing rules and protocol … and the result is plain to see – they have acquired both honour and wealth.

(*Shprikh enters.*)

SHPRIKH : Ah! Afanasy Pavlovich, what a surprise! Well, I'm very glad, I didn't expect to meet you.

KAZARIN : Ditto. Is this a social visit?

SHPRIKH : Er – yes. And yours?

KAZARIN : Ditto.

SHPRIKH : Really. But it is fortunate that we met – I wanted to discuss some business with you.

KAZARIN : You have always been preoccupied with business – for the first time it appears it will be business-like.

SHPRIKH : A *bon mot*! You never miss one! But in fact, this is serious.

KAZARIN : I need to be serious with you as well.

SHPRIKH : So we can manage to be amicable then –

KAZARIN : I doubt it. But speak.

SHPRIKH : Allow me to ask you then: have you heard anything to the effect that your friend Arbenin – (*He makes horns on his head with his fingers.*)

KAZARIN : What? Quite impossible! Are you certain of it?

SHPRIKH : Good Lord, I've just been settling things myself just five minutes ago. What could be more certain?

KAZARIN : The devil ever picks his moment!

SHPRIKH : You see, his wife the other day – I can't remember exactly when – at a ball or in church or possibly at the masquerade – met with a little Princey. He found her quite attractive, and promptly he was loved and happy. Then without any warning, the minx decided to refuse what was between them. The Prince, breathing fire and fury, flew round the whole world, telling everybody what had happened between them – a sure way to excite scandalous consequences. I was asked to damp the business down. Of course, I was glad to, and everything was smoothed over. The Prince promised to keep quiet. He wrote her a note, and here I am, the humble messenger, with it – or with my slightly improved version of it.

KAZARIN : Take care the husband doesn't tweak your nose.

SHPRIKH : I've been in much more dangerous situations than this and managed to avoid a duel.

KAZARIN : And no-one ever thrashed you?

SHPRIKH : As always, you come out with your badinage. I can tell you that I'm not one to risk my life without good reason.

KAZARIN : Indeed? And a life so valued by everyone shouldn't be risked for less.

SHPRIKH : Well, we'll let that pass. May I talk to you about my important business?

KAZARIN : What is it?

SHPRIKH : A *bon mot*! No, the matter concerns –

KAZARIN : We'll have to let it pass, too – Arbenin is coming.

SHPRIKH : No, there's nobody. Count Vruti sent me five borzoi dogs –

KAZARIN : Your anecdote is really quite amusing.

SHPRIKH : Now I know you're a hunter. You might like to buy these dogs.

KAZARIN : So, Arbenin – duped…

SHPRIKH : Listen –

KAZARIN : Taken in, fooled, laughed at! There are the fruits of marriage for you.

SHPRIKH : You would have been glad of this opportunity –

KAZARIN : When people say marriage brings happiness –
it's all lies! Don't get married, Shprikh.

SHPRIKH : I've been married for years. Listen, one especially
is a treasure.

KAZARIN : One wife?

SHPRIKH : One dog!

KAZARIN : Oh, you're still on your dogs. Listen, my dear
friend, one can never tell what God will send. I don't
know about your wife, but you won't get rid of your dogs
to me. (*Arbenin enters with a letter. Kazarin and Shprikh
are standing by the bureau, so he does not see them. He is absorbed by the letter.*) See! He's absorbed. He's got the letter.
It would be interesting to know what is in it.

ARBENIN : That's the thanks I receive. Hardly have I saved
his honour and his future, without even knowing who he
is – or what he is … oh! Snake! – unheard-of treachery –
just for fun he strolled into my house and poisoned it with
shame and disgrace. I can't believe my eyes. I've forgotten
all the lessons of my own past. I have been like a child,
innocent of the world, not even suspecting such repul-
sive behaviour. I thought it was all her fault … I thought
he doesn't know who this woman is … he will forget the
night's adventure as a dream. But he hasn't forgotten, he's
still looking for her. And now he's found out who she is,
he still can't stop himself. That's my thanks! I have wit-
nessed a good deal in my life, but still I find this shocking.
(*He reads the letter again.*) 'I found you, but you didn't want
to confess.' This is only conventional modesty. 'You are
right … what can be worse than the rumours of gossips?
Anybody might have been eavesdropping. So it was not
scorn that I read in your passionate eyes, but fear.. You
prefer secrecy, and this will be our secret. I would rather
die than take a refusal from you.'

SHPRIKH : The letter! Well, well – indeed. There will be a
disaster.

ARBENIN : Oh, such a skilful seducer – I would send him a reply stained with blood. (*He sees Kazarin.*) Ah, you're here.

KAZARIN : I've been waiting an hour for you.

SHPRIKH (*aside*) : I will fly to the Baroness. She will be compelled to take steps, which will put her in my debt. (*He goes out unnoticed.*)

KAZARIN : Shprikh and I ... oh, where is Shprikh? He's disappeared. (*Aside*) The letter! This is it! Now I think I understand! (*To Arbenin*) You are abstracted.

ARBENIN : Yes, I'm contemplating.

KAZARIN : The futility of hope and earthly bliss?

ARBENIN : Almost – gratitude.

KAZARIN : Well, there are many opinions on that subject. And whether one thinks this or that about it, the thing itself is certainly worthy of meditation.

ARBENIN : What is your opinion?

KAZARIN : I think, my dear friend, that gratitude depends mostly on the value of the favour given. Kindness is not always regulated by intention. For example, yesterday I won about five thousand roubles from Slukin, and I can honestly say that I feel deep gratitude to him. Whether I'm drinking, or in bed, or eating my fill, I'm still thinking about him.

ARBENIN : As usual, you are being clever, Kazarin.

KAZARIN : Listen, I love you, my friend, and will talk seriously to you. But please, for God's sake, get rid of that austere and lowering air of yours. I can open for you all the secrets of worldly wisdom. If you want to hear my opinion of gratitude, I can give it to you. Please, just be patient. Whatever Voltaire or Descartes may say, for me, the world is a pack of cards, life is the bank, Fate is dealing and I'm playing. So I use the laws of gambling in life. For example, if I put a thousand roubles on an ace – for no reason, just because of a premonition – ah! in cards

I'm superstitious – and purely by chance, and without any cheating, my opponent wins, I may accept that, but I won't feel any gratitude to my ace. I'll take my luck in silence, but then I'll cheat and cheat tirelessly until I've made it even. Then of course I'll hide the card which I've been cheating with under the table. Now – but aren't you listening, brother?

ARBENIN (*thoughtfully*) : Evil is everywhere – everywhere there are cheats. And I, like a dolt, just listened to how it all happened.

KAZARIN (*aside*) : He's still abstracted. (*To him*) Now we will proceed to another case, and bring it to light, but gradually so as not to lose our way. Imagine, for example, that you wanted to go back to gambling and pleasure seeking, and your old partner came to you and said, 'Be careful, my dear sir,' and favoured you with a great deal of worthless advice, and you, for some strange reason, accepted it and blessed him and wished him long life and so on and so on … Or imagine if he restrained you from the bottle … then the best way to show gratitude for that would be to get him drunk without any more ado, and then to sit at cards with him till you've bankrupted him. That's real gratitude for some advice, and if he 'saves' you from losing the game … then go to the ball and fall in love with his wife … or, if you can't fall in love with her, at least seduce her – just to show your gratitude for her husband's benevolence. In either case you would be right, my friend, for only that would teach him a lesson for the lesson he tried to teach you.

ARBENIN : You are a famous moralist|! (*Aside*) So, everybody now knows about it. So, Prince … I will teach you, lesson for lesson.

KAZARIN (*not paying attention*) : I must explain one other point. Suppose you love a woman. For her sake, you sacrifice honour, wealth, friendship, life itself perhaps. You surround her with entertainment and compliments. But why should she feel gratitude to you? You've done it out of your passion, and partly out of egotism. You sacrificed everything – not to give her happiness, but to possess her. And really, if you think about it cool-headedly, you will agree that nothing in this world is absolute.

ARBENIN (*looking upset*) : Yes, yes, you're right. What does a woman find in love? She needs new conquests every day … you can weep, be tormented, plead with her, but she'll find your miserable voice and your appearance laughable. You are right: the man who tries to find earthly paradise in a woman is a fool.

KAZARIN : Now you're talking sense, even though you're married and happy.

ARBENIN : Am I?

KAZARIN : Are you not?

ARBENIN : Oh, happy … yes …

KAZARIN : I'm very glad. But it still seems a pity that you got married!

ARBENIN : Why?

KAZARIN : Well … I remember the old days … we were fellows with our wits about us – though we'd drink till our wits were out! Those were the days! In the morning we'd stay in bed, dreaming languidly about the previous night. Then dinner – wine – sent up by Raoul … the wine bubbled and sparkled in the goblets, there was argument, repartee, good humour … then to the theatre – I'm trembling just remembering it – how the two of us would go backstage, and lure a dancer or an actress each for the night … don't you agree that our life in those days was better – and cheaper? Or, after the play was over, we'd go straight to one of our favourite dens and start gambling. By the time we'd arrive, the game would be in full swing – on the cards you'd see piles of gold roubles. It was clear that real life was here, though there was always at least one person paler than a corpse in the grave. We would sit down, and that's when the battle would commence. Here, here, you experienced thousands of emotions and feelings rushing through your soul. Often outrageous schemes would clutch at your brain, and if you won by them, if you subjugated Fate till she was under your foot, then even Napoleon himself seemed pitiable and ridiculous.

ARBENIN : Oh, who can take me back? Oh, my passionate hopes, my intolerable fiery days, who can bring you back to me? For you I would forego the bliss of my new life. I would give away my leisure and serenity – they're not for me. Am I fit to be a husband and the head of a family when I have experienced the sweet flavour of dissipation and sin, and never trembled to meet them? No! Be gone, virtue, I renounce you, I've been fooled by you, and our short alliance I hereby break. Farewell, farewell.

(*He falls onto the chair and covers his face with his hands.*)

KAZARIN : Now he is mine!

Scene Three

Prince Zvezdich's room. There is an open door leading to an inner room where the Prince can be seen asleep on the sofa. The servant looks at the clock.

SERVANT : It's only just past seven o'clock, and he ordered me to wake him at eight. He sleeps like a real Russian, not *à la fashion*. I think I've got time to run up to the shop. I can lock the door … I think that'll be best … oh, somebody's on the stairs … Ah, I'll say he's not at home, then I can be free.
(*Arbenin enters.*)
ARBENIN : Is the Prince at home?
SERVANT : Nobody's at home.
ARBENIN : That's not true.
SERVANT : He went out five minutes ago.
ARBENIN (*listens carefully*) : You're lying. He's here. (*Pointing to the inner room*) And I'll wager he's asleep, and dreaming sweetly. Listen to his breathing. (*Aside*) But soon he will stop.
SERVANT (*aside*) : He doesn't miss anything. (*To Arbenin*) The Prince will not permit that he is wakened.
ARBENIN : He likes to sleep … So much the better for him. Soon he will have to sleep eternally. (*To Servant*) I think I have already told you that I will wait until he awakens. (*The Servant goes, leaving Arbenin alone.*) Now, what a convenient moment – now or never … Now I can do it without fear, easily. I will prove that in our generation

there is at least one soul in whom inflicted injury brings forth the fruit of revenge. No, I am not their slave, it's too late for me to bend my knee before them. In the past they would have laughed at me if I had challenged an enemy. They won't laugh now. No, that is not me. I will tolerate no more disgrace, not even for an hour. (*He looks through the door.*) He is sleeping! ... What does he see in this last dream of his life? (*He smiles cruelly.*) One blow will finish him – his head is hanging already, I will help the blood run out of it ... it will be for the good of mankind. (*He enters the room. A pause. He returns, pale.*) I can't do it! (*Silence.*) Yes! It's beyond my will, beyond my power. I couldn't keep faith with my own self, I trembled for the first time in my life. Am I a coward? ... a coward ... who said that? I did myself, and it is the truth. Wretched, wretched – a frightened, shameful, despised man. Our modern sensibility has prostrated you – you're no different from everyone else. You were just a braggart in front of yourself. Oh, such a pity ... truly a pity ... even you have been worn down by the load of modern enlightenment. Love – you weren't able to love ... revenge – you came here for revenge ... but you couldn't achieve that either. (*Silence. He sits down.*) I flew too high. I must choose the surer way ... a different idea surges in my tormented brain now ... Very well, he will live. Stabbing is not the enlightened method any more – stabbers are executed in the public squares. I was bred among enlightened people – gossip and money ... these are our daggers, our poison.

(*He takes pen and ink and writes a note, then picks up his hat. He goes to the door and collides with a lady in a veil.*)

LADY IN VEIL : Oh! Everything will be ruined ...

ARBENIN : What's that?

LADY (*breaking from him*) : Let me go.

ARBENIN : No – this is not the pretend protest of easy virtue. (*To her, austerely.*) Be silent! Not a word, otherwise this moment … what a suspicion! Draw up your veil, here, while we're alone.

LADY : I've mistaken – this is the wrong place.

ARBENIN : You've mistaken the time, but not the place.

LADY : Oh, for God's sake, please let me go, I don't know you.

ARBENIN : Your alarm aggravates my suspicion … draw up your veil. He's asleep … but he may wake at any moment. I know everything … but I want to be certain.

LADY : You know everything!

(*He draws up her veil, then steps back in surprise.*)

ARBENIN (*recovering himself*) : I thank you, Fate, for allowing me, at least for the present, to be mistaken.

LADY : What have I done? Now everything is finished!

ARBENIN : Despair does not suit this moment – though I admit that it is hardly agreeable to meet at such a time, not fiery embraces, but this cold hand. It was only momentary fear … nothing else … I'm not assuming anything, I shall be glad to stay silent about this – be grateful for that – and grateful that it's me and nobody else … otherwise the whole town would be cackling about it.

BARONESS : Oh, he is awake, I can hear him talking.

ARBANIN : In his delirium … but compose yourself, I'm leaving now. Only explain to me – by what power has Cupid bewitched you? Why are all women passionately in love with this heartless numbskull? Why is he not at your feet with pleading eyes, oaths and tears? Yet you – you come here alone. But you are a woman with a soul. You have forgotten your shame, you have come here to give yourself to him – why? Another woman, who is no worse than you, is also ready to give everything for him – her happiness, life, love … just for one word from him, one glance … why? Oh, I'm going out of my wits … (*Frenziedly*) Why? Why?

BARONESS (*decisively*) : I understand what you are talking about. I know why you are here.

ARBENIN : How? Who told you? (*Realizing he has said too much.*) And what do you know?

BARONESS : Oh, I implore you, please forgive –

ARBENIN : I didn't accuse you – just the opposite, I rejoice in this fellow's fortune.

BARONESS : I was blinded by passion. I was guilty in everything. But listen –

ARBENIN : Why? – I – really – it doesn't matter to me. I am an enemy of strict morality.

BARONESS : If it were not for me, there would have been no letter, and neither –

ARBENIN : Oh, this is too much, really … Letter! … Which? Ah, then it was you, you were the pandar – you taught them. Do you often play that role? What makes you do it? Do you bring your innocent victims here? Do young people approach you? Oh, I'm sure you must be absolutely indispensable in fashionable drawing rooms … but the fornication of our ladies doesn't shock any more.

BARONESS : Oh, my God …

ARBENIN : I'm talking to you quite frankly. Tell me, how much are you paid for it?

BARONESS (*falls into the armchair*) : You are merciless.

ARBENIN : Oh, I have made a mistake, I apologize – obviously you do it for nothing but sheer pleasure. (*He makes to go.*)

BARONESS : Oh, I will go out of my mind … Please, wait, he is coming … no, he isn't … oh, I will die …

ARBENIN : Very well, go on with your intrigues – this one will heighten your reputation. Don't be afraid of me. Farewell. But please God we never meet again … You have torn from me everything I have in this world, and if ever I see you again, whatever or wherever we are, I will hound you … whether it's in the streets when you're all alone … or in the glitter of society … if our paths cross again, then it will be the worse for you. I would have killed you, but death is a gift which I must reserve for another. As you see, I am merciful – and instead of the torments of hell, I leave you your earthly paradise. (*He goes.*)

BARONESS (*calls after him*) : Listen – I swear … it was a lie … She's innocent … and the bracelet … it was me – it was only me … He has gone, he can't hear me. What can I do? Everywhere there is despair … there's no need … I will save him, whatever the cost. I will humiliate myself, I will reveal my deception, my perfidy. He's getting up, he's coming. I will screw up my courage. Oh, this is agony!

PRINCE (*from the next room*) : Ivan! Who's there? … I thought I heard voices! What kind of people are these? They don't even let you have half an hour for a nap. (*He enters.*) This is an unexpected visit. How beautiful! I am glad to see you. (*Baroness turns round to him. Prince starts.*) Oh, Baroness! No … impossible!

BARONESS : Why did you start? (*In a weak voice*) Are you surprised?

PRINCE (*embarrassed*) : Of course, but – er – you're welcome too … I wasn't expecting such a pleasure.

BARONESS : It would be strange if you had been expecting it.

PRINCE : What did I think? Oh, if only … I know –

BARONESS : You might have known everything, but in fact you know nothing.

PRINCE : I'm glad to correct my mistake. I will accept whatever punishment you think is fitting. I was blind and dumb not to be aware of making a mistake, and now I can't find the right words. (*He takes her by the hand.*) Your hand is as cold as ice. I can see suffering in your face. Do you doubt what I say?

BARONESS : You are still making a mistake. I haven't come here to make love or to listen to passionate declarations. And I didn't come to forget my fear and shame. No, I've come out of holy duty. My old life is over, a new life awaits me now. It was I who caused all this mischief, and now I'm abandoning society for ever, I've come to make some amends. I came here to lay bare my disgrace. I haven't saved myself from shame … but I will save someone else.

PRINCE : What do you mean?

BARONESS : Please, don't interrupt. It cost me a great effort to come here to speak to you. Though you're not aware of it, you yourself are the cause of my suffering. Yet I must still save you. What for? Why? I don't know. Perhaps you don't deserve this sacrifice … You couldn't love or understand me, and perhaps I wouldn't want that anyway. But listen – today I found out – how? It doesn't matter – I found out that yesterday you imprudently wrote a letter to Arbenin's wife. And, according to rumour, she loves you in return. But it isn't true, it's not true. Don't believe it, for goodness' sake. Oh, the very thought – it will murder us, all of us. She knows nothing, but her husband read your letter, and he is dangerous either in love or hatred. He has already been here, and he will kill you. He is steeped in vice … and you are so young.

PRINCE : Please don't be afraid. Arbenin knows the ways of society, and he is too clever to allow rumours to spread or to let an affair like this, without any aim or purpose, run to a bloody conclusion. But if he is angry, don't be alarmed – Le Page will supply us with pistols, thirty-two paces will be measured out and – I didn't win these epaulettes by fleeing in the face of the enemy.

BARONESS : But if somebody cherishes your life more than you, if your life has a connection with another life, and if they kill you … kill you, oh my God! And I am the cause of everything.

PRINCE : How?

BARONESS : Please, have mercy –

PRINCE (*having thought*) : I am obliged to accept a challenge. I know that to him I am guilty. I injured his honour, though not knowingly, so there is no other way that I can exonerate myself.

BARONESS : There is one way.

PRINCE : I can tell a lie? Is that what you would suggest? You must find another way than that. I cannot lie simply to preserve my life. I shall go now, and make my challenge.

BARONESS : Please, wait a moment, listen to me. (*She takes his hand.*) You are all fooled. That mask – (*she tries to support herself on the chair, but falls back into it*) – it was I!

PRINCE : You? Oh, heavens – (*Silence.*) But Shprikh – he said – he is guilty of all this –

BARONESS (*sitting up and recomposing herself*) : It was a momentary delusion. It was a strange madness, and now I regret it. And it's over. Please forget it completely. Return the bracelet to her. It was found by pure coincidence, by a curious chance. And please promise me that the truth will be kept secret. God will judge my behaviour. He will forgive you – and it is not for you to grant me forgiveness. I am going away soon. I do not think we shall ever meet again. (*As she approaches the door, she sees that he wants to run to her.*) Please, don't follow me. (*She goes out.*)

PRINCE (*after long contemplation*) : What can I think? The only thing I'm sure of is that like a stupid schoolboy I've missed a heaven-sent opportunity. (*He comes to the table.*) And what's this? A note … who from? Arbenin … I'll read it. 'My dear Prince, Would you care to come to X's house this evening? There will be plenty of … and we shall all have a good time … I don't want to wake you – otherwise you would spend the whole evening yawning. I will expect you tonight. Yours sincerely, Yevgeny Arbenin.' Mmm … it would take a very sharp eye to see bullets in this. Whoever heard of inviting one's enemy to supper before challenging him to a duel?

Scene Four

The room at X's. Kazarin, the owner of the house and Arbenin at a card table.

KAZARIN : It seems that you have abandoned that whimsical attachment to matrimony which society usually honours, and have stepped straight back into your old ways. Congratulations, brother ... You must be a poet, indeed judging by all the signs, a genius – for, obviously, domestic life stifles your spirit. Give me your hand, my dear friend. You are ours.

ARBENIN : I am yours. I have abandoned every shred of the married man's way of life.

KAZARIN : I must be honest and admit my pleasure at that – and at discovering how clever people view things nowadays. Obviously, respectability is worse than imprisonment for them. Are we going to be partners?

OWNER : We have to pluck the Prince's feathers.

KAZARIN : Yes yes. (*Aside*) This will be most amusing.

OWNER : We shall see. (*A noise is heard.*) I raise you three times.

ARBENIN : It's him.

KAZARIN : Your hand is shaking.

ARBENIN : It's nothing. I'm out of practice –
 (*Enter the Prince.*)

OWNER : Ah, Prince, I am very honoured – please come in – we are all equal here, take off your sword of rank. Pray be seated. This will be a battle royal!

PRINCE : Oh, I shall be very happy just to watch.

ARBENIN : Are you still afraid to play cards after that other incident?

PRINCE : I'm not afraid to play with you. (*Aside*) According to the rules of my game, I should flatter the husband when bewitching the wife … the most important thing is to win there – so I must lose here. (*He sits at the table.*)

ARBENIN : I went to your place today –

PRINCE : Yes, I read your note, and as you see I am obedient.

ARBENIN : I met someone at the door who was most embarrassed – and alarmed.

PRINCE : Did you recognize them?

ARBENIN (*laughing*) : I think I did! Prince, you are a dangerous seducer. I understood everything and drew my own conclusions about you.

PRINCE (*aside*) : He hasn't understood anything, it's obvious. (*He goes to the side and puts down his sabre.*)

ARBENIN : I really would be most anxious if you were to cast your eye on my wife.

PRINCE (*casually*) : Why?

ARBENIN : Well – I fear I lack the attributes which lovers cherish most in the husbands of their mistresses. (*Aside*) He's not even embarrassed. I will destroy your sweet world, you fool, and I will add some poison. If you would put your soul on one card, I'd stake mine against it. (*They play. Arbenin is the banker.*)

KAZARIN : Fifty roubles.

PRINCE : And me.

ARBENIN : Let me tell you a little story which I heard when I was younger. Somehow it keeps running in my head. Once upon a time there was a married man – your card wins, Kazarin – and this married man trusted his wife without any ifs or buts: he lived in a dream of sweet innocence. You are too attentive to the story, Prince – it would be better to concentrate on the game. You could lose a lot.

This husband was loved in return, so that day followed day in tranquillity and bliss. And to complete the idyll, this happy husband found a true friend. He had done this man a substantial favour, and he – the friend – was known to be honourable and trustworthy. And what do you think happened? I can't remember how or when, but the husband discovered that this honourable and noble friend, his earnest debtor, had offered his services to the wife.

PRINCE : And what did the husband do?

ARBENIN (*ignoring the question*) : Prince, you have forgotten the game. You're playing your cards without looking at them. (*Stares at him piercingly.*) And do you know what the husband did? He invented an excuse, and then slapped him. Well, what would you have done in his place, Prince?

PRINCE : Oh – the same … And then did they offer each other satisfaction with pistols?

ARBENIN : No.

KAZARIN : With sabres?

ARBENIN : No no.

KAZARIN : So they made up?

ARBENIN (*smiling bitterly*) : Oh no –

PRINCE : What did he do then?

ARBENIN : He felt he had had his revenge, and the seducer was left with the slap.

PRINCE (*laughing*) : But that's against all the rules.

ARBENIN : Oh. Then will you please tell me where the book is which sets out the rules on how to hate or how to take revenge? (*They play. Silence.*)

PRINCE : The left wins, the left wins!

ARBENIN (*getting up*) : Wait a moment. You have changed this card.

PRINCE : Me? Please –

ARBENIN : That's the end of the game. There's no decency here. You – (*breathing hard*) – you are a scoundrel, a cardsharp!

PRINCE : Me? Me?

ARBENIN : A scoundrel. And I will brand you so that nobody will dare to be seen with you. Here! (*He throws the cards into his face. The Prince is dumbfounded. Quietly*) Now we are quits.

KAZARIN : What's the matter with you? (*To the owner of the house*) He's gone berserk at the crucial moment. The Prince was just getting excited. He stood to lose at least two hundred thousand roubles.

PRINCE (*coming back to himself, jumps up*) : Very well – follow me, follow me! Blood! Only blood will wash away this insult!

ARBENIN : A duel? With you? Me? You've chosen the wrong man.

PRINCE : You are a coward! (*He makes to leap on him.*)

ARBENIN (*thunderously*) : Very well, I am a coward. But I warn you – don't come any closer to me. And I advise you not to stay here any longer. I am a coward – but you are not capable of frightening even a coward.

PRINCE : I'll make you fight a duel. I'll publish details of your behaviour everywhere, and I'll make it plain who the scoundrel really is.

ARBENIN : A good idea.

PRINCE (*coming closer*) : I will tell everybody that your wife – now, be careful! … remember that bracelet!

ARBENIN : You have just been punished for that.

PRINCE : What? This is madness! Where am I? Set the whole world against me? I'll kill you!

ARBENIN : You certainly can – but let me give you a word of advice – kill me straightaway. Otherwise, your courage, which is so formidable now, will begin to blow away.

PRINCE : But what's become of my honour? Please give me the name back, please give it back to me, and I will kneel at your feet. But you are without principle, … are you a human being or a demon?

ARBENIN : Me? I'm a gambler.

PRINCE (*falling down and covering his face*) : Oh, my honour, my honour!

ARBENIN : You will never regain your honour. The dividing line between good and evil has been rubbed out, and the whole of society will dismiss you with contempt. From now, your road will be that of a pariah, you will drink the syrup of bloody tears, and the happiness of those nearest to you will only multiply the pain in your soul. That one thought will possess your mind night and day. And gradually the knowledge of love, the knowledge of beauty, will shrivel and die, and nobody will have the skill to comfort you. Your comrades and cronies will fall away from you like leaves from a rotten twig, and you will pass through crowds ashamed, hiding your face, and burning with a remorse greater than that of the criminal for his crime. So – farewell. (*Leaving.*) I wish you a long life.

(*Arbenin goes out.*)

ACT THREE

Scene One

At the ball.

HOSTESS : I was expecting the Baroness. I don't know whether she's coming or not, but it will be a pity if she doesn't.

1 GUEST : I don't understand –

2 GUEST : Are you waiting for Baroness Shtrall? She's gone away.

GUESTS : Where? What for? How long ago?

2 GUEST : To the country – today, this morning.

A LADY : Dear God! Whatever for? Did she choose to go?

2 GUEST : Her head was brimming with fantasies – it's all these novels, such airy fairy nonsense.
(*They disperse. A group of men are seen.*)

3 GUEST : Did you hear that Prince Zvezdich lost at cards?

4 GUEST : On the contrary, he won. But it appears he did it by cheating, which is why he's had it.

5 GUEST : Did he offer a duel?

4 GUEST : No, he didn't dare to.

3 GUEST : What a scoundrel he proved himself.

5 GUEST : From today, I don't want to know him.

6 GUEST : Nor I! I think it's terrible behaviour –

4 GUEST : Is he going to be here?

3 GUEST : I doubt whether he would venture here –

4 GUEST : Here he is!

(*Prince enters. Hardly anybody greets him. Everybody moves away, except 5 and 6 Guests, who stare at him rudely, then they too move away. Nina is sitting on a sofa.*)

PRINCE : She and I have been left alone. There will be no second chance. (*To her*) I must speak with you briefly, and you must listen.

NINA : I must?

PRINCE : Yes, for the sake of your own happiness.

NINA : What a strange sympathy you have for me.

PRINCE : Well, it's strange that it is you who are the cause of my social death. But I feel pity for you. I can see that I have been struck by the same hand as that which will kill you. But revenge is beneath me. But please listen to me: take care. Your husband is a villain. He is without soul, without God, and I feel sure that trouble is threatening you. Please be careful. Farewell. The villain has not yet been exposed, so that he can't be given his deserts yet, but the day will come, and I'll wait for it … Please, take your bracelet – I don't want it any more.

(*Arbenin is watching them from a distance.*)

NINA : Prince, you are moonstruck. It's not even worth being angry with you.

PRINCE : Please be careful. I am seeing you for the last time.

NINA : Where are you going? Far away? Not to the moon, though?

PRINCE : No, closer. To the Caucasus. (*He goes.*)

HOSTESS (*to guests*) : Now, almost everybody is here, and I hardly think this room will hold us all. Would you please proceed to the ballroom, ladies and gentlemen? Gentlemen, this way please. *Mesdames*, there.

(*They depart, leaving Arbenin alone.*)

ARBENIN : I had doubts? Me? While everybody else is sure of it. I catch hints everywhere. Oh, they find me pitiable and ridiculous. And where are the fruits of my experience – or that power which in times past I could use to conquer the crowd with a casual witticism? Two women killed it. One of them – oh, I love her, love her – and I am so beguiled – but no, I will never surrender her to them. They are not our judges. I will be the judge, and I will carry out the awful sentence. I will find a suitable means of execution for her, while the real execution will be here (*indicating his heart*). She will die. I can't live with her any more. But to live apart? (*As if frightened by the thought*) It is concluded: she will die. And I will not deviate from this my firm resolve. So she was doomed to die in the blossom of her life, just as she was doomed to be loved by a villain such as I … and to love someone else. It is clear! … How can anyone be permitted to live after that? Oh, thou God, unseen but omniscient, take her, take her. I give her to Thee as a pledge. Forgive her, and bless her. But I'm not God, that's why I can't forgive her. (*Music is heard. He paces round the room and suddenly stops.*) One night, ten years ago, when I was sinking in the quicksands of self-indulgence, I lost everything down to my last rouble. In those days, though I knew the value of money, I didn't know the value of life. I was in despair. I went out and bought a phial of poison. I returned to the gambling table. The blood was boiling in my breast. In one hand I held a glass of lemonade; in the other, four spades. The last rouble was in my pocket, alongside the poison. The stakes were at the highest. But Fate rescued me, and in an hour I had won everything back. But ever since, through all the anxieties of a laborious life, I've kept that powder, kept it as a talisman, something mysterious and powerful, for the black moment which is almost here.

(*He walks away. The hostess, Nina, ladies and gentlemen have entered.*)

HOSTESS : What a relief to pause for a moment.

A LADY : It's so hot, I shall melt away.

A GENTLEMAN : Nastasya Pavlovna might sing something
    for us.
NINA : But there are no new songs, and the old ones have
    become tedious.
A LADY : Oh please, Nina, sing something for us.
HOSTESS : Do be kind, don't make us go on pleading with
    you.
NINA (*sitting at the piano*) : But you must be extremely at-
    tentive – that will be my revenge on you for your in-
    sistence!
    (*She sings.*) When I see thy tears are flowing
            There is no pain for me,
        For then I know my hated rival
            Brings not bliss to thee.

        A worm there is who gnaws unceasing
            At thy earthly store,
        And I rejoice to see his failure
            To adore as I adore.

        But if thine eye were once to glisten
            With a gladsome tear,
        Then would bitter anguish taunt me
            And hell invest its fear.
    (*During the third verse, Arbenin enters and leans over the pi-
    ano. Seeing him, she stops.*)
ARBENIN : Why stop? Continue –
NINA : I have forgotten the end.
ARBENIN : If you wish, I can remind you of it.
NINA (*embarrassed*) : No, why? (*To the hostess*) I am not well.
    (*She rises.*)
1 GUEST (*to another guest*) : Every modern song has words
    in the last verse which a young lady simply cannot utter.
2 GUEST : Besides, our native language is so direct that it is
    really not suitable for a lady's ear.

3 GUEST : How very true! Our proud language does not
    bend – it's like a savage, it's not a slave. It's we who are
    slaves – we who slavishly bend backwards.
    (*They are given ice cream. The guests drift into different rooms,
    till Arbenin and Nina are left alone. The Stranger appears at
    the back of the stage.*)
NINA (*to the Hostess*) : I feel so hot, I would like to sit down
    and rest for a while. (*To Arbenin*) My angel, would you
    bring me an ice cream?
    (*Arbenin starts, then goes for the ice cream. As he returns, he
    sprinkles powder on it.*)
ARBENIN : Now death help me.
NINA (*to him*) : I feel so depressed and restless – as though
    some dark trouble were looming.
ARBENIN (*aside*) : Premonitions are sometimes true. (*Giving
    her the ice cream.*) Take this. It will be the perfect remedy
    for your restlessness.
NINA : Ah, this will cool me.
ARBENIN : Of course it will.
NINA : It's all so empty here.
ARBENIN : What would you prefer? If the emptiness de-
    presses you, you can rouse yourself by watching people's
    follies and vices. They are what makes this world go
    round.
NINA : You are right – it's terrible.
ARBENIN : Yes, terrible!
NINA : There are no innocent souls here …
ARBENIN : No. I thought I'd found one but – alas – it was
    not so.
NINA : What are you talking about?
ARBENIN : I said I thought I had found an innocent soul –
    you.
NINA : You are pale.
ARBENIN : I've been dancing too much.

NINA : Stuff and nonsense, *mon ami.* You have sat out the whole evening.

ARBENIN : Then I must be pale because I didn't dance enough.

NINA (*giving him the empty dish*) : Please take this – could you put it on the table?

ARBENIN (*taking it*) : Everything, everything! She didn't leave a drop for me! How cruel! (*Thoughtfully*) I have taken the fatal step. There is no returning now. But no-one else must share her death. (*He throws the dish on the floor. It breaks into pieces.*)

NINA : How clumsy of you.

ARBENIN : Never mind. I feel ill – let's go home now.

NINA : Certainly. But please tell me, my dear – you are in such a black mood. Are you displeased with me?

ARBENIN : No. Tonight I have been pleased with you. (*They go.*)

STRANGER (*alone*) : I nearly took pity on her – there was one moment when I wanted to rush forward … (*Thoughtfully*) No, let Fate take its course. The time will come for me to join in.

(*He goes.*)

Scene Two

At Arbenin's: the bedroom. Enter Nina, followed by her maid.

MAID : Madame, you are pale tonight.

NINA (*taking off her earrings*) : I'm unwell.

MAID : You are tired.

NINA (*aside*) : My husband frightens me, I don't know why. He is sad, and seems so far away. (*To Maid*) It's stifling in here. I'm out of breath – I think it must be my corset. Tell me, did my dress suit me tonight? (*She goes to the mirror.*) You're right, I'm very pale, pale like death. But then – who is not pale in Petersburg? Except the old princess – but that's only her make-up. What a hypocritical society. (*She takes off her hairpiece and wraps away her plait.*) Put that away, and will you pass me my wrap? (*She sits in an armchair.*) How delightful that new waltz was! I was enjoying dancing so much – the hypnotic rhythm carried my spirit far far away, and my heart shrank, not from sadness, and not exactly from happiness. Sasha, please pass me my book. Oh, how that Prince pesters me. But I feel sorry for him, too, he's such a foolish boy! What he told me tonight – villain, deserts … Caucasus … it's gibberish … what a shame …

MAID (*indicating the dress*) : Shall I take it away?

NINA : No, leave it.

(*Nina is deep in thought. Arbenin appears at the door.*)

MAID : Shall I go?

ARBENIN (*quietly, to the Maid*) : Yes, go. (*The Maid stays where she is.*) I said, you may go. (*Maid goes out. Arbenin locks the door.*) You don't need her any more.

NINA : Is it you?

ARBENIN : Yes, it is.

NINA : I think I am unwell – my head is burning. Come close to me. Give me your hand. Do you feel how hot my hand is? But why did I have that ice cream? Perhaps I caught a cold from it. Do you think so?

ARBENIN (*inattentively*) : Ice cream? Yes …

NINA : My dear, I wanted to talk to you. You have changed recently. I miss your old tenderness. Your voice is sharp and you seem so far away. It's all happened since that masquerade! I've sworn to myself that I will never go to another.

ARBENIN (*aside*) : That won't be difficult. You can do without them from now.

NINA : It's a lesson to me for behaving so thoughtlessly.

ARBENIN : Thoughtlessly? Oh!

NINA : That's what the trouble was.

ARBENIN : Then you should have thought, beforehand.

NINA : If I'd known you had moods like this, I would never have become your wife, to torment you, and to suffer so much myself. Oh! It's so amusing, so very jolly!

ARBENIN : Really? And what is my love to you?

NINA : Love? Is this love? I don't need a life like this.

ARBENIN (*sitting by her*) : Yes, you are right. What is life? Life is worthless. While the warm blood of youth still runs in your veins, everything in life seems happy and pleasant. But the time of passion and desire passes away, and everything becomes darker and darker. What is life? That's a well-known children's riddle. First, there's birth; then, the dreary sequence of doubts and torments; and last, death. All that, everything – lies.

NINA (*indicating her breast*) : Something is burning me here.

ARBENIN (*continuing*) : It's not important – it will stop. Be silent, and listen to me. I said that life seems precious while it is still young, but how long does that last? Life is like hell – while you're waltzing, it's amusing and everything is bright and clear. But when you return home and take off your crumpled dress, all that is forgotten, and you only feel fatigue. It's better to take your leave of life while you're young, before your soul has compromised with the soulless emptiness of life. It's better to go to the life beyond while the fight with death is so easy. That is a happiness not given to all.

NINA : No no, I want to live.

ARBENIN : Why? What for?

NINA : Yevgeny, I am suffering, I am ill.

ARBENIN : And do you think there are no sufferings worse than that?

NINA : Will you send for the doctor, please?

ARBENIN : Life goes on for ever – death lasts just one moment.

NINA : But I want to live.

ARBENIN : And do you know the consolations that await a martyr?

NINA (*frightened*) : I beg you, please send for the doctor.

ARBENIN (*gets up, coldly*) : I won't do it.

NINA (*after a pause*) : You are joking, of course, but it is a heartless joke. I could die – please, send quickly.

ARBENIN : So what? Can't you die without a doctor?

NINA : That's cruel, Yevgeny. I am your wife.

ARBENIN : Yes, I know – I know.

NINA : Please, have mercy. Everything is burning in my chest. I'm dying.

ARBENIN : So quickly? Not yet. There is still half an hour left.

NINA : Oh, you don't love me.

ARBENIN : Why should I love you? Because you planted a hell in my heart? No, I am glad, I am glad you are suffering. My God, how can you demand love? Tell me, was my love not enough for you? Did you know the value of my tender feelings for you? Did I expect much in return for my love? Only a smile, a tender smile, or a kind look from you. And what have I had? Intrigue and infidelity. Is it possible to betray me for one kiss from that idiot? When I would be glad to surrender my soul at your behest? To betray me? Me? And so soon!

NINA : If only I knew my fault, I would –

ARBENIN : Don't say any more, or I'll lose my wits! When will these agonies end?

NINA : The Prince found my bracelet – and then you were tricked by some tittle-tattler.

ARBENIN : No – I was tricked! Enough! … I was mistaken, I dreamt that I could be happy, I imagined that love and loyalty could be mine … but the fatal hour is here, and everything is void as the diseased babblings of delirium, Perhaps I could have fulfilled my dreams, while belief lasted, perhaps I could have revived everything which had once blossomed in my heart … But you didn't want that – you – weep, weep – really, what are, Nina, what are woman's tears? Water! But I have really wept, me, a man. Yes, I've wept – from bitterness, from spite, jealousy, shame and torment. And you don't know what it is for a man to weep. At that moment, avoid him – death is in his hands, and hell in his heart.

NINA (*falls on her knees in tears, and raises her hands to the sky*) : Oh Lord God, have mercy! He doesn't hear, but Thou hearest all. Thou knowest all, and in Thine omnipotence Thou wilt vindicate me.

ARBENIN : Stop it! At least don't lie to God!

NINA : But I'm not lying. I would not profane Him with false prayers. I give my suffering soul to Him, who is your Judge, but my Protector.

ARBENIN (*pacing the room with folded arms*) : Yes, it is time for you to pray, Nina. You must die in a few minutes, and your death will be a mystery to everyone. Only God's judgment will judge me.

NINA : What? To die! Now, at this moment – no, it cannot be –

ARBENIN (*laughing*) : I knew you would be fearful of the moment –

NINA : Death, death! He is right – oh, my breast is agony – this is hell –

ARBENIN : Yes. At the ball, I gave you poison.
(*Silence.*)

NINA : I don't believe it. It cannot be. No, you are just teasing me. (*She runs to him.*) You are not a villain … No … in your soul there is a spark of good … you can't kill me like that, cold-bloodedly, when I am so young. Don't turn away, Yevgeny, don't – please, stop my torment. Save me. Dispel my fear. Look at me. (*She looks into his eyes, then jumps away.*) Oh! I can see death in your eyes. (*She falls on the chair, and closes her eyes. He comes up to her, and kisses her.*)

ARBENIN : Yes, you will die, and I will stay here alone, alone. The years will pass, I will die, but I will still be alone. That is terrible. But you – fear not. A beautiful world will open before you, and angels will guard over you. (*He weeps.*) Yes, I love you, I love you … I tried to forget everything. There is a limit to my revenge – here, look: your murderer is here, weeping before you like a child.

NINA (*starts up, withdraws from him*) : Here, here! … please, help … I'm dying … poison, it's poison … Oh, nobody hears – I understand, you have been careful … there's nobody … nobody's coming. But remember, there is a God who judges. And my dying word is: Curse you, you murderer! (*She runs towards the door, but falls before she reaches it.*)

ARBENIN (*laughing bitterly*) : Curses! What use are curses? I've been cursed by God. (*He comes to her.*) You poor creature, this punishment was too hard on you. (*He stands with folded arms.*) She is pale. (*He shivers.*) But all the features of her face are calm, serene. I can read in them neither remorse nor regret. Have I … ?

NINA (*in a weak voice*) : Farewell, Yevgeny … I am dying, but I am innocent … and you are the evil one.

ARBENIN : No no, don't say that. Nothing can help you now, neither lies nor cunning. Tell me now, at the last – have I been tricked? (*Silence.*) Hell itself could not jest at my love as you did. You are silent? So my revenge is just. You are beyond help, you will die, and the cause of your death will be a mystery – be sure of that.

NINA : It doesn't matter now, but before God I am innocent.

(*She dies. Arbenin comes to her, then quickly turns away.*)

ARBENIN : Lies.

(*He falls into the armchair.*)

ACT FOUR

Scene One

Arbenin sits on a sofa by the table.

ARBENIN : The truceless war within my soul, this baleful struggle, has made me weak. I have found peace now, yes, but such a wearying and deceiving peace. Occasionally I am wracked again in this icy dream, but now my heart is aching as if it were waiting for something. Is everything not finished yet? Are there more earthly sufferings for me to taste? … Clouds of nothing … The days will pass dully by, and oblivion will come – the burden of years will crush my imagination. One day my heart will be still. (*He falls into thought, then suddenly raises his head.*) I was mistaken. No, this memory is merciless! I see her pleas and grief so vividly. Oh, be still, awakened serpent.
(*He drops his head into his hand. Enter Kazarin.*)
KAZARIN (*quietly*) : Is Arbenin here? Ah, yes – but quiet. He is grieving, and sighing. Let us see what comedy he will play now. (*To him*) My dear friend, when I heard of your sorrow, I immediately wanted to see you. But – well – it's Fate, every person has his own sufferings. (*Silence.*) Enough of this, brother – take off the mask, don't lower your eyes so magnificently – that's for other people, for the public – but we're both actors, aren't we? … tell me, brother … oh, you really look pale, as if you'd been at cards all night. Oh, you cunning old fox – we shall have to have our little chat

about this later. Here are your relatives: of course, they've come to pay their last respects to the dead. Goodbye – till we meet again!

(*Kazarin goes out. Enter relatives.*)

A LADY (*to her niece*) : You can see God's curse on him. He was a bad husband and a bad son. Remind me to buy material for a black dress. My income isn't much nowadays, but I still have to waste money on relatives.

NIECE : What was the cause of your cousin's death, *ma tante?*

LADY : The cause was the stupidity of our society. It will make trouble for you as well.

(*They go out. From the room of the dead Nina, enter the Doctor and an old man.*)

OLD MAN : Did she pass away in your presence?

DOCTOR : No, they didn't manage to find me in time. I've always said that one shouldn't mix ice cream and dancing.

OLD MAN : Did you see how rich and ornate the decorations were? Last spring, when my brother was buried, the coffin was decorated in the same way.

(*He goes out.*)

DOCTOR (*coming to Arbenin and taking his hand*) : You should rest.

ARBENIN (*starts*) : Ah! (*Aside*) Oh, my heart shrank!

DOCTOR : I think you are indulging your grief too much. Go now, and sleep.

ARBENIN : I'll try.

DOCTOR : There's nothing more to be done. You need to take care of yourself.

ARBENIN : Oh, I'm invulnerable. Whatever I've suffered in this world, I've always survived. I wished for happiness, and God sent it to me in the shape of an angel, but my foul breath desecrated this divinity. This beautiful creature is still here – but look, cold and dead. Once in my life I saved someone whom I hardly knew, I saved him from annihilation – and thoughtlessly, laughingly, without so much as a by-your-leave, he stole from me my all, all – and so quickly.

(*He moves away.*)

DOCTOR : He is seriously ill, I have no doubt. His thoughts are swamped with anguish. If he loses control of his mind, I could not vouch for his life.

(*Going out, he runs into the Stranger and the Prince who are entering.*)

STRANGER : Excuse me – is it possible to see Arbenin?

DOCTOR : I really can't say – his wife passed away yesterday.

STRANGER : I'm sorry.

DOCTOR : And he is in the depths of grief.

STRANGER : I'm sorry for him, too. Is he at home?

DOCTOR : He? At home? Yes.

STRANGER : I have something important for him.

DOCTOR : You are one of his friends, I suppose?

STRANGER : Not yet, but we've come here in the hope of making friends.

DOCTOR : He is seriously ill.

PRINCE (*anxiously*) : Is he confined to bed? Unconscious?

DOCTOR : No, he's still walking about and talking – there is still hope.

PRINCE : Thank God. (*The Doctor goes out.*) At last –

STRANGER : You appear flushed. Are you still resolute in your decision?

PRINCE : Are you still sure that your suspicion is justified?

STRANGER : Listen, we both have the same aim, we both hate him, but you don't know his soul – it is sombre and deep as the entrance to the grave. And whoever the doors open for will be buried within eternally. Suspicion must suffice for proof. For he knows neither forgiveness nor sympathy. When he is crossed, he must revenge. That is what spurs and guides him. Her early death cannot be mere chance. Now, since you and I are both his enemies,

I'm glad to be of service to you. If you achieve your duel, I shall be near to witness it.

PRINCE : But how did you find out that I had a grievance against him just yesterday?

STRANGER : I would be glad to enlighten you, but it would take too long. Besides, the whole town is talking about it.

PRINCE : What an intolerable thought!

STRANGER : It is vexing you too much.

PRINCE : You don't know what shame is.

STRANGER : Shame? – No – and you will learn to forget it as you get more experience of life.

PRINCE : But who are you?

STRANGER : Do you need my name? I am your collaborator. I defended your honour zealously, eagerly. You don't need to know anything more … Listen! Somebody's coming. The step is heavy and slow – it's him. Yes, it's certainly him. Please, withdraw for a moment. I must speak to him. We don't need you as a witness now.

(*The Prince steps aside. Enter Arbenin with a candle.*)

ARBENIN : Death! Death! That word has penetrated everything here. I'm sated with it. It persecutes me. I stared at her dumb corpse, speechlessly, while time passed, and my heart was full, full of inexpressible grief. Her features were suffused with serenity and childish innocence. An eternal smile bloomed on her face when the doors of eternity opened before her and her soul read its destiny. Have I made a mistake? No, it's impossible – who could prove her innocence to me? – false, false. Where are the proofs? I have the proofs. If I didn't believe her, who could I believe? Yes, I was a passionate husband, but a cold judge. And who would dare dissuade me from my conviction ?

STRANGER : I will dare!

ARBENIN (*startled, he steps back and brings the candle up to his face*) : And who are you?

STRANGER : It's not surprising, Yevgeny, that you don't
recognize me. We used to be friends.
ARBENIN : But who are you?
STRANGER : I'm not a good angel. Yes, unnoticed, I've been
with you everywhere, always changing my face, always
in different clothes. I know your every deed, even your
thoughts sometimes – it was I, only a few days ago, who
warned you at the masquerade.
ARBENIN (*taken aback*) : I don't like prophets! … I must ask
you to leave immediately. I am serious.
STRANGER : Of course you are. But in spite of your fearsome voice and your firm demand, I won't leave. I can
see that you didn't recognize me; but I'm not one of those
whom a moment of danger can deflect from a long-fixed
purpose. I have reached my goal, and I may perish here,
but I will not take one single step towards leaving.
ARBENIN : I'm like that myself – but it's not something to
boast about. (*He sits down.*) I'm listening.
STRANGER (*aside*) : Up to now my words haven't touched
him. Have I been mistaken? We shall see. (*To him*) Seven
years ago you wouldn't have failed to recognize me, Arbenin. I was young then, inexperienced, passionate and rich.
But already in those days, your heart was icy cold, even
then you were vindictive, haughty … devilish contempt for
everything you were so proud of. I don't know – should I
ascribe it to your intellect or your circumstances? – I won't
discuss it now: your soul can be understood only by its
creator – God!
ARBENIN : Well, that's a fine beginning!
STRANGER : I can promise you the end is no less fine!
Once – I found you persuasive, you attracted me; my
purse was full of gold, and I believed in Fate. I sat down
to play with you, and lost. My father was a miser and a
tyrant. So in order to avoid his reproaches, I decided to
try my fate once more. Although you were young, too,

you held me in your claws, and again I lost everything. I plunged into despair, perhaps you remember the tears, the prayers … but in you they stirred up only laughter. Oh, it would have been better if you had simply stabbed me to death – for had you been a prophet then, you could have seen what lay in store for you: only now is your evil seed being harvested. (*Arbenin tries to rise, but slumps back in thought.*) I had to abandon everything from that moment, everything – women and love, the joys of youth, sweet dreams and the beating of affection – and a different world opened up for me, a world of alien feelings, the world of the pariah, of empty souls and frigid passions and tormenting nightmares. I realized that money was tsar of the earth, and I had fallen before it. Years passed. I lost everything – health and wealth. And for ever before me the doors of happiness were barred. I made a last compact with my fate, and I became as you see me now. Ah, you are trembling – you understand my purpose now, and you know what I am going to tell you. Yes, now say again that you don't recognize me.

ARBENIN : Leave my house – I did recognize you – I did!

STRANGER : Leave your house! Is that all? You laughed at me, and now it's my turn to laugh at you. Recently a rumour reached my ears that you were happy, rich, married – and bitterness overcame me. My heart murmured, and for a long time I could only think: why? Why is he happy? And the voice inside me whispered: Go! Go, and disturb him! So I started following you, mingling in the crowds of people. I followed you everywhere, and at last my efforts were crowned. Listen! I discovered one fact – and – and – I will disclose it to you … (*slowly*) Listen: you … killed … your wife!

(*Arbenin starts. Prince comes forward.*)

ARBENIN : Killed? I? Prince … oh, what's happening …

STRANGER (*stepping back*) : I have told my part. The rest is his.

ARBENIN (*in frenzied agitation of mind*) : Ah, it's a plot …
very well … I am in your hands … what's holding you
back? Nothing … you are the tsars here … and I am humble – I am now at your mercy … my soul recoils from your
looks … I am a fool, a child, I can't find the answer to your
accusation. I have been conquered in a single moment,
baffled as by a riddle. So I will put my head on your block
without any fuss. But haven't you miscalculated? I am
still master of myself, and of my experience and strength.
You thought she had taken all that with her to the grave.
And you thought I wouldn't be able to pay you as I would
have in the past, in my best days. So that's the low opinion of me you had because of the vicious gossip of the
mob! Yes, this scene has been well rehearsed. But you
haven't guessed its denouement. This young boy – even he
wants to try conclusions with me. One humiliation wasn't
enough for him – now he wants another! You'll get it, my
boy! Life bores you? That's not surprising – that's how
it is for nincompoops and cheap philanderers. Console
yourself – you'll be killed – and you'll die with the name
of scoundrel still on you.
PRINCE : We shall see – but please, make haste.
ARBENIN : Yes, come on, come on.
PRINCE : At last, I'm satisfied.
STRANGER (*getting between them and the door*) : Yes – but you
have forgotten the most important thing –
PRINCE (*stopping Arbenin*) : Oh yes. You must understand one
more thing – that you accused me falsely, that your victim
was not guilty … You were too quick to insult me – I was
on the point of telling you the truth … so now, come on!
ARBENIN : What? What?
STRANGER : Your wife was innocent – you were too harsh
on her.
ARBENIN (*laughs*) : Oh yes, you have a joke for every occasion.

PRINCE : No no, it's not a joke. I swear to God that the
bracelet was found by pure chance, the Baroness picked
it up, and she gave it to me. I was fooled myself. But your
wife scorned my love. If I had known at that moment
that from that little mistake so much wickedness would
sprout, I would never have chased her glance or her smile.
It will all be clear to you from this letter, written by the
Baroness. Read it quickly – time is precious.
(*Arbenin takes the letter and reads.*)
STRANGER (*raising his eyes to heaven hypocritically*) : Prov-
idence punishes the sinner! The innocent has died – so
tragically! Sadness and bitterness were her earthly lot,
but beyond the earth salvation awaits her! Yes, I saw her,
her eyes showed clearly the purity of her soul. Who could
have guessed that this enchanting flower would be blasted
by a single thunderbolt? Why are you silent? Tear your
hair, torment yourself and scream – horrible, it's horrible!
ARBENIN (*rushes at them*) : I will strangle you, murderers!
(*Suddenly he loses his strength and collapses into the armchair.*)
PRINCE (*trying to pull him up*) : Remorse won't help you.
Pistols are waiting for us – our difference hasn't been settled yet. He is speechless, he's not listening. Has he lost
his wits?
STRANGER : Perhaps.
PRINCE : You blocked my course.
STRANGER : We were aiming at the same target, but from
different angles. I got my revenge – for you, I fear it is
too late!
ARBENIN (*rises with mad looks*) : What did you say? It's un-
bearable, unbearable! I was so insulted, I was so sure …
Please, forgive me, oh my lord, forgive me (*He laughs.*) her
tears, her complaints, her pleadings – did you hear them?
(*He kneels.*) Here, I have fallen on my knees before you: tell
me, please tell me – treachery and intrigue are obvious –
I want – demand – that now you prove the accusations

against her, at this moment. Is she innocent? Have you been here? Have you looked into my soul? As I am asking you now, so she asked me. It was a mistake – I made a mistake – did I? She told me it was, but I said she was lying. (*He gets up.*) I told her she was. (*Silence.*) That's what I must impress on you. I'm not her murderer. (*He stares hard at the Stranger.*) You – confess. At once. Have the courage to speak. To open with me at least. Oh, my dear friend, why were you so cruel? I truly loved her – if in paradise she sheds one tear, I shan't forgive heaven for it. But you I do forgive. If she were to shed a tear, I would not forgive. (*He falls on the Stranger's breast, and weeps.*)

STRANGER (*pushing him away, roughly*) : Come on – pull yourself together. (*To the Prince*) Let's take him out of here … He'll soon recover in the open air. (*He takes his hand.*) Arbenin!

ARBENIN : We will be apart for eternity. Farewell .. come on … come on … here – here –
(*He pulls himself free, and rushes through the door towards Nina's coffin.*)

PRINCE : Stop him!

STRANGER : Now this proud mind is rent.

ARBENIN (*coming back with a wild moan*) : Look here! Here! (*He runs to the middle of the room.*) I told you, you were cruel!
(*He falls to the floor, half sitting, half lying, with dull eyes. Prince and Stranger stand over him.*)

STRANGER : I've been seeking revenge for so long. This is it.

PRINCE : He is mad … and happy. And I? I have for ever lost my peace of mind, and my honour.

The End

About the Translators

Valentina Hine was born and educated in the former USSR and is now based in the UK. She is a freelance researcher and translator, whose work has been featured in major television productions, including Thames Television's 1991 documentary series on Chernobyl and Central Television's 1989–1993 series which included the film "Hello, Do You Hear Us?" produced by the Soviet Latvian-born director, Joris Podnieks in collaboration with the Soviet-British Creative Association. Behind the scenes, she has contributed translations and subtitles for Border-line Productions and London-based television studios. Beyond broadcasting, her translation projects in creative media have fostered cross-cultural dialogue between Russian and British cultural institutions. In addition to her freelance work, she has also been involved in higher education, serving as a language assistant at the University of Birmingham and a seminar tutor at Aston University.

Robert Leach is a retired academic, a writer and a freelance theatre director. He held senior positions at Birmingham and Edinburgh Universities, and his published work includes biographies, travel books and books of theatre history and theatre theory. His *Theatre Workshop: Joan Littlewood and the Making of Modern British Theatre* (Exeter University Press, 2006) and his two-volume *Illustrated History of British Theatre and Performance* (Routledge, 2019) were both shortlisted for Theatre Book of the Year. He has also translated plays by Sergei Tretyakov, which were published by Glagoslav

Publications in 2019. His professional theatre work has included acting in the USA and directing in Moscow, where he staged the Russian premiere of the formerly-banned *I Want a Baby* by Sergei Tretyakov.

Glagoslav Publications Catalogue

- *The Time of Women* by Elena Chizhova
- *Andrei Tarkovsky: A Life on the Cross* by Lyudmila Boyadzhieva
- *Sin* by Zakhar Prilepin
- *Hardly Ever Otherwise* by Maria Matios
- *Khatyn* by Ales Adamovich
- *The Lost Button* by Irene Rozdobudko
- *Christened with Crosses* by Eduard Kochergin
- *The Vital Needs of the Dead* by Igor Sakhnovsky
- *The Sarabande of Sara's Band* by Larysa Denysenko
- *A Poet and Bin Laden* by Hamid Ismailov
- *Zo Gaat Dat in Rusland* (Dutch Edition) by Maria Konjoekova
- *Kobzar* by Taras Shevchenko
- *The Stone Bridge* by Alexander Terekhov
- *Moryak* by Lee Mandel
- *King Stakh's Wild Hunt* by Uladzimir Karatkevich
- *The Hawks of Peace* by Dmitry Rogozin
- *Harlequin's Costume* by Leonid Yuzefovich
- *Depeche Mode* by Serhii Zhadan
- *Groot Slem en Andere Verhalen* (Dutch Edition) by Leonid Andrejev
- *METRO 2033* (Dutch Edition) by Dmitry Glukhovsky
- *METRO 2034* (Dutch Edition) by Dmitry Glukhovsky
- *A Russian Story* by Eugenia Kononenko
- *Herstories, An Anthology of New Ukrainian Women Prose Writers*
- *The Battle of the Sexes Russian Style* by Nadezhda Ptushkina
- *A Book Without Photographs* by Sergey Shargunov
- *Down Among The Fishes* by Natalka Babina
- *disUNITY* by Anatoly Kudryavitsky
- *Sankya* by Zakhar Prilepin
- *Wolf Messing* by Tatiana Lungin
- *Good Stalin* by Victor Erofeyev
- *Solar Plexus* by Rustam Ibragimbekov
- *Don't Call me a Victim!* by Dina Yafasova
- *Poetin* (Dutch Edition) by Chris Hutchins and Alexander Korobko

- *A History of Belarus* by Lubov Bazan
- *Children's Fashion of the Russian Empire* by Alexander Vasiliev
- *Empire of Corruption: The Russian National Pastime* by Vladimir Soloviev
- *Heroes of the 90s: People and Money. The Modern History of Russian Capitalism* by Alexander Solovev, Vladislav Dorofeev and Valeria Bashkirova
- *Fifty Highlights from the Russian Literature* (Dutch Edition) by Maarten Tengbergen
- *Bajesvolk* (Dutch Edition) by Michail Chodorkovsky
- *Dagboek van Keizerin Alexandra* (Dutch Edition)
- *Myths about Russia* by Vladimir Medinskiy
- *Boris Yeltsin: The Decade that Shook the World* by Boris Minaev
- *A Man Of Change: A study of the political life of Boris Yeltsin*
- *Sberbank: The Rebirth of Russia's Financial Giant* by Evgeny Karasyuk
- *To Get Ukraine* by Oleksandr Shyshko
- *Asystole* by Oleg Pavlov
- *Gnedich* by Maria Rybakova
- *Marina Tsvetaeva: The Essential Poetry*
- *Multiple Personalities* by Tatyana Shcherbina
- *The Investigator* by Margarita Khemlin
- *The Exile* by Zinaida Tulub
- *Leo Tolstoy: Flight from Paradise* by Pavel Basinsky
- *Moscow in the 1930* by Natalia Gromova
- *Laurus* (Dutch edition) by Evgenij Vodolazkin
- *Prisoner* by Anna Nemzer
- *The Crime of Chernobyl: The Nuclear Goulag* by Wladimir Tchertkoff
- *Alpine Ballad* by Vasil Bykau
- *The Complete Correspondence of Hryhory Skovoroda*
- *The Tale of Aypi* by Ak Welsapar
- *Selected Poems* by Lydia Grigorieva
- *The Fantastic Worlds of Yuri Vynnychuk*
- *The Garden of Divine Songs and Collected Poetry of Hryhory Skovoroda*
- *Adventures in the Slavic Kitchen: A Book of Essays with Recipes* by Igor Klekh
- *Seven Signs of the Lion* by Michael M. Naydan

- *Forefathers' Eve* by Adam Mickiewicz
- *One-Two* by Igor Eliseev
- *Girls, be Good* by Bojan Babić
- *Time of the Octopus* by Anatoly Kucherena
- *The Grand Harmony* by Bohdan Ihor Antonych
- *The Selected Lyric Poetry Of Maksym Rylsky*
- *The Shining Light* by Galymkair Mutanov
- *The Frontier: 28 Contemporary Ukrainian Poets - An Anthology*
- *Acropolis: The Wawel Plays* by Stanisław Wyspiański
- *Contours of the City* by Attyla Mohylny
- *Conversations Before Silence: The Selected Poetry of Oles Ilchenko*
- *The Secret History of my Sojourn in Russia* by Jaroslav Hašek
- *Mirror Sand: An Anthology of Russian Short Poems*
- *Maybe We're Leaving* by Jan Balaban
- *Death of the Snake Catcher* by Ak Welsapar
- *A Brown Man in Russia* by Vijay Menon
- *Hard Times* by Ostap Vyshnia
- *The Flying Dutchman* by Anatoly Kudryavitsky
- *Nikolai Gumilev's Africa* by Nikolai Gumilev
- *Combustions* by Srđan Srdić
- *The Sonnets* by Adam Mickiewicz
- *Dramatic Works* by Zygmunt Krasiński
- *Four Plays* by Juliusz Słowacki
- *Little Zinnobers* by Elena Chizhova
- *We Are Building Capitalism! Moscow in Transition 1992-1997* by Robert Stephenson
- *The Nuremberg Trials* by Alexander Zvyagintsev
- *The Hemingway Game* by Evgeni Grishkovets
- *A Flame Out at Sea* by Dmitry Novikov
- *Jesus' Cat* by Grig
- *Want a Baby and Other Plays* by Sergei Tretyakov
- *Mikhail Bulgakov: The Life and Times* by Marietta Chudakova
- *Leonardo's Handwriting* by Dina Rubina
- *A Burglar of the Better Sort* by Tytus Czyżewski
- *The Mouseiad and other Mock Epics* by Ignacy Krasicki

- *Ravens before Noah* by Susanna Harutyunyan
- *An English Queen and Stalingrad* by Natalia Kulishenko
- *Point Zero* by Narek Malian
- *Absolute Zero* by Artem Chekh
- *Olanda* by Rafał Wojasiński
- *Robinsons* by Aram Pachyan
- *The Monastery* by Zakhar Prilepin
- *The Selected Poetry of Bohdan Rubchak: Songs of Love, Songs of Death, Songs of the Moon*
- *Mebet* by Alexander Grigorenko
- *The Orchestra* by Vladimir Gonik
- *Everyday Stories* by Mima Mihajlović
- *Slavdom* by Ľudovít Štúr
- *The Code of Civilization* by Vyacheslav Nikonov
- *Where Was the Angel Going?* by Jan Balaban
- *De Zwarte Kip* (Dutch Edition) by Antoni Pogorelski
- *Głosy / Voices* by Jan Polkowski
- *Sergei Tretyakov: A Revolutionary Writer in Stalin's Russia* by Robert Leach
- *Opstand* (Dutch Edition) by Władysław Reymont
- *Dramatic Works* by Cyprian Kamil Norwid
- *Children's First Book of Chess* by Natalie Shevando and Matthew McMillion
- *Precursor* by Vasyl Shevchuk
- *The Vow: A Requiem for the Fifties* by Jiří Kratochvil
- *De Bibliothecaris* (Dutch edition) by Mikhail Jelizarov
- *Subterranean Fire* by Natalka Bilotserkivets
- *Vladimir Vysotsky: Selected Works*
- *Behind the Silk Curtain* by Gulistan Khamzayeva
- *The Village Teacher and Other Stories* by Theodore Odrach
- *Duel* by Borys Antonenko-Davydovych
- *War Poems* by Alexander Korotko
- *Ballads and Romances* by Adam Mickiewicz
- *The Revolt of the Animals* by Wladyslaw Reymont
- *Poems about my Psychiatrist* by Andrzej Kotański
- *Someone Else's Life* by Elena Dolgopyat
- *Selected Works: Poetry, Drama, Prose* by Jan Kochanowski